0

Eyes On The True Light

Thank You, Jesus!!!
And thanks to my Mom, who was willing to help
find answers to my crazy questions!

~ Elivia Kanatiguilli

There is a pronunciation guide in the
back of the book for clarity on the character's
names and certain phrases.

Letter from the author.

I write this letter, because in the book you are about to read, certain grammar rules of the English language have been purposely disregarded. These said rules are stated below along with the reason of why. I want everyone to understand that I am a Christian and hold strongly to my Faith in Christ. If something goes against what I believe, —no matter what it is— I will not go along. I believe if you compromise in one area —even something small— you will end up continuing to compromise and then it'll become something really big. I understand that my opinion is not what everyone else thinks, nor will I coerce anyone into agreeing with me. I only ask that people exercise wisdom and take time to really research anything questionable.

1: As a Christian, I believe there is only one True God. He is the Holy Trinity —Father, Son, and Holy Spirit. He is three in One. Any name of a false god, I will not capitalize. I believe capitalization to be a sign of recognition and honor. I will not capitalize the name 'satan'. He has no power and deserves zero honor. Nor will I capitalize words such as death, hell, demon, etc. I will only honor my God, the Creator of Heaven and earth.

2: In the same way, I refuse to call a person 'lord', 'master', etc. I will not capitalize most titles (governor, president, king, etc.) unless it is part of the person's name.

3: I will not capitalize the names of false religions. Religions such as catholicism, buddhism, etc. are not true according to the Bible. Most church denominations I also will not capitalize. You are either Christian or you're not; there is no in between.

(The only time these may be capitalized is at the beginning of a sentence.)

4: Church will be capitalized when referring to the Body of Christ.

5: To give emphasis, I sometimes capitalize words such as hand, voice, breath, etc. when referring to that of God's. Any pronoun referring to God I will capitalize. I also capitalize certain words such a joy, faith, love, trust, etc. to show emphasis when talking about Trust in God or God-given Love (etc.). This is not always but most of the time (depending on context and point). All attributes of God are capitalized.

6: When saying the Name of Jesus or Jesus' Name, "name" will always be capitalized. It is His Name and He is my Savior.

7: As a sign of respect, I often capitalize 'mom' or 'dad' if someone is talking about their parents.

Other notes and facts—

1: I use person-first language. So, I would say this person has (name disability). I believe people should not be known by any disability they may have. Also, God can heal anything and we do not want to claim any disease. Say "I have a headache" not "my headache".

2: In any book I write, if you see the word "Indian", it does not refer to Native Americans. It NEVER will. Indians are people of or from India. Columbus called us that believing he had reached the Indies. It would have been fine had people corrected the mistake as soon as they realized, but they did not. We have been called something we are not since Europeans came to the Americas. It is both offensive to us and to true Indians. They're not Choctaw Indians; they're the Choctaw Native American Tribe. We are not Indians; we are **NATIVE AMERICANS.**

These things I have spoken unto you, that in Me ye might have peace. In the world ye shall have tribulation: but be of good cheer; I have overcome the world. ~ John 16:33

Part 01: Pioneer

Chapter 01: False Accusations

Casting all your care upon Him; for He careth for you.
~01 Peter 05:07

"Hey, how long does it take to groom a horse?!"

Rawad Ditka ran a hand over the Gypsy Vanner mare's now-clean coat. He dropped the wide brush back into his bucket of grooming supplies before looking up at his co-worker. "You need me for something?"

Liam shook his head in mock annoyance. "Is there ever a time when you pay attention to more than just the one horse?" Liam knew him well. They had been friends since the beginning of high school. And, when Liam's parents died, Rawad's parents had fought to get custody of him. The two had been brothers ever since.

Rawad grinned. "If I'm not grooming a horse."

Liam rolled his eyes.

"Did you need me?" Rawad repeated his earlier question.

"Yeah, the hay shipment's here."

"Cool. Be there in a sec. Soon as I get the grooming brushes put away."

Liam nodded and left.

Rawad put his grooming bucket in the tack room before hurrying outside.

"Mommy, when is Daddy coming home?"

Madison Levine turned to smile at her daughter. "He should be home soon. Once he gets home, we'll eat supper."

"Can we listen to music while we wait??"

"Yes, of course." Madison grabbed her phone off the kitchen counter. She opened her music folder and selected the shuffle play. She turned up the volume a little before laying the phone back on the counter.

While her daughter ran to get a coloring book, she turned off the stove. Her daughter came back to the kitchen and sat at the small table with her coloring book.

Madison watched her daughter. Kyrsten, who was seven, had just finished first grade; she had passed her finals with flying colors. She was young, but she retained information easily. She already loved to read, and she loved to listen to Christian music. It amazed Madison how well Kyrsten could memorize the lyrics to the songs.

Lights flashed through the kitchen window, and Madison heard the garage door start to open.

Kyrsten heard it too, and she looked up from her coloring book excitedly. "Daddy's home!!"

Madison nodded. "Go put your coloring book and pencils away before he comes in. We'll need to eat here soon."

Kyrsten grabbed her coloring supplies and hurried upstairs with it.

Madison was setting plates on the table when her husband walked in and hugged her from behind. "Hey, there," he said.

"Hey." Madison turned to embrace him. "How was your day?"

They could hear Kyrsten running down the stairs.

"Good." Grinning, Justin took two steps back toward the kitchen breezeway. He mouthed, *One, two, three,* as he lifted a finger for each silent number. On three, they heard, "Daddy!!" Justin dropped his left hand and spun to lift their daughter into his arms. "Hey, Sweet Girl!"

Madison smiled and grabbed silverware to set on the table. She cleared her throat. "Supper's ready."

"After supper, can I show you my new picture?" Kyrsten asked her daddy.

"Of course. I would love to see it!"

Though he was still grinning, Madison could see the lines around his eyes. She heard stress underneath the cheer in his tone.

"Hey, see you tomorrow!" Liam waved to Rawad as he passed by on his way out.

"Yep," Rawad replied. He hurried outside to his SUV. He checked the inwardly facing watch on his wrist and winced. He was late. *Really* late. Carrie would not be too happy.

He started his vehicle and drove home. Hopefully, his daughter would not be in bed, yet. He didn't think she would be. In all reality, they would be finishing supper right about now.

Ten minutes later, Rawad pulled into his driveway and parked. He got out and hurried into the house. His daughter, Anissa, met him in the hallway.

"Daddy, you're late," she informed him.

"I know; I'm sorry." He bent down to hug the nine-year-old. "Did y'all already eat?"

"Yes. Mommy put yours in the oven."

"Okay. Let's go in there." He walked with Anissa to the kitchen.

"I am so sorry. I realize how late I am."

Anissa sat down at the table and watched her parents silently.

Carrie pulled a plate of food out of the toaster oven before turning to face him. "I'm not mad. It's not like you do this alot or anything." She shrugged. "Just don't be late again."

"What? No hello?" Rawad teased.

Carrie set his plate on the table across from where Anissa sat. She perched a hand on her hip. "You're the one who walked in here and greeted me by talking about how sorry you are. Assuming you wanted a response to that right away, I figured I'd say 'hello' after you decide to greet me like a normal person."

Rawad laughed. "Hello, it's nice to see you." With mock formality, he continued, "And I must say, you are looking especially lovely this evening." He stepped closer and put his arms around Carrie. "How's that for a greeting?"

Carrie grinned widely. "Hello, Rawad. I'm glad you're home."

Rawad kissed her. "Look at Anissa," he whispered before pulling away. While talking to Carrie, he had been watching their daughter out of the corner of his eye. When she thought neither parent was paying attention, Anissa had picked up her dad's plate and set it in the place beside her. Rawad thought it was cute.

Carrie looked at Anissa. "Did you move your daddy's plate?"

Anissa grinned. "I wanted to sit beside him."

Rawad rounded the table and sat down beside her. "How's this?"

"Good." Smiling, she gave a single nod.

"Night, Mommy."

"Good night, Kyrsten." Madison turned her daughter's bedroom light off on her way out. She closed the door behind her. With a soft sigh, she walked down the steps.

Justin was already seated on the end of the couch when she entered the living room. He motioned for her to take the seat across from him.

Justin didn't wait for her to ask what was going on. "Two serious things happened at work today." He paused.

"Okay." Madison was worried by his scared expression.

"Do you want the not great news or the terrifying news first?"

Alarm covered Madison's face. "Just tell me what happened, Justin."

"First off, I was fired, just before quitting time today."

"Why??"

Justin held up a cautioning hand. "I'm getting there." He took a deep breath before continuing his story. "Some men approached me today as I was clocking out. They were from the sheriff's department. They asked me to talk to them privately before coming home."

Madison tensed in her seat. This couldn't be good.

Justin hesitated. "I've been accused of fraud and identity theft. They said they have evidence. I have a week to prove my innocence. They said if I can provide alibis for the times they gave me, I'll be okay. If I can't prove my innocence, I will be sent to prison for a few years."

"Dear Jesus, help us," Madison whispered. "I can't believe this. Why would they think you are the guilty person? You're the most honorable man I know! And you've been working at the DMV for seven years!"

"They don't care how long I've been there. Plus, they said that the crime was committed from my computer."

Madison got up and sat beside him on the couch. "Let's pray. We'll figure this out. We'll prove your innocence, and it'll all be alright."

Friday, May 22

"Daddy, can I go to work with you, today?" Kyrsten had just come downstairs looking for her father.

"Actually, Daddy is staying home with us today!" Madison breezed into the living room and took the seat next to Justin.

"Really?!" Excitement lit Kyrsten's eyes. "Yayyy!" She clapped her hands once in delight.

Justin grinned.

"Oh, I forgot!" Kyrsten rushed out of the room to get something from her room.

Justin glanced at Madison. "She sure is excited this morning."

Madison chuckled. "Yeah! She's so sweet. God did an amazing job creating her."

Kyrsten came back into the living room and presented her dad with a flyer.

Justin took it. "What's this?"

Kyrsten lost no time in telling him. "It's for horse riding. You, me, and Mommy need to go ride on their new trail!"

"Oh, that's right." Madison glanced at the flyer Justin still held. "A local stable built a new trail for horseback riders on their property. They're inviting families to come check it out. They said anyone coming before the 30th would be provided with horses and any necessary gear from the stable at half the price."

"We should go, Daddy. I've never ridden a horse." Kyrsten stated matter-of-factly.

"We might not be able to go, Sweetheart." Madison bit her lip.

Justin handed the flyer back to Kyrsten. "How about you keep this for now. If your mom and I can find a good day, we'll do it."

"Yes!!!" Kyrsten jumped in excitement. She left the room again, Justin assumed to put the flyer away.

"With everything going on, should we go do that? We could wait till you're cleared, then take her riding." Madison sounded worried.

Justin shook his head. "What if I'm not cleared?? You know that happens alot. I want to spend as much time as I can with her now. Just in case. I didn't commit the crime, but I don't know how to prove that, yet."

They sat in silence for a few moments. Justin's phone ringing all the sudden made them both jump. Justin snagged it off the coffee table and looked at the screen. "Hello?" he answered. He didn't recognize the number, but it had an Alabama area code.

"Hello. Is this Justin's number?" The girl on the other end sounded friendly.

"Who is this?"

"Kathlyn Shirah."

"What? Wow. I haven't heard from you in awhile."

"I know. I talked to your mom on the phone a few days ago, and she gave me your number."

"So, what's life been like for you the past couple years?"

"So, I live in Shorter, now. I opened a stable here last month, and I'm still figuring out how to make that work."

Justin chuckled. "You always did love horses."

"You got that right."

"Who is that?" Madison whispered to him.

Kathlyn, my cousin, he mouthed.

They talked for a few more minutes before Justin said goodbye and hung up the phone.

"Did you say that was your cousin?" Madison asked.

"Yeah. Her name is Kathlyn. I haven't seen her in years. She lives down in Shorter now."

Madison nodded. "I'll go grab my computer, and let's see if we can figure out how to clear you."

Justin agreed. "My computer is over there if you want to grab it instead."

Chapter 02: Faith Of A Child

And said, Verily I say unto you, Except ye be converted, and become as little children, ye shall not enter into the kingdom of heaven. ~Matthew 18:03

"Wake up, Sweetheart." Madison gently shook her daughter awake.

Kyrsten opened her eyes. "Good morning, Mommy," she whispered.

"Hey, you want to get up and get ready to go? We have to leave for church soon."

Kyrsten sat up quickly. "Okay!" She got out of bed as Madison left the room.

Once she was dressed, Kyrsten hurried down the steps. When she entered the kitchen, she saw her dad sitting at the table working on his computer. "Daddy!" She threw her arms around him.

"Good morning, Sweet Girl. Did you sleep well?" Justin hugged her close.

Kyrsten nodded. "What are you doing on your conputer?"

"*Computer*," Madison corrected gently.

"*Compewter*," Kyrsten repeated.

Madison smiled. Normally, Kyrsten did not have trouble with that word.

"I am checking on something for work." Justin answered his daughter's question.

Kyrsten crossed her arms thoughtfully. "Daddy, it's Sunday. God says not to work."

Justin chuckled. "He does, huh? I guess you're right."

Kyrsten frowned. "I'm right," she assured him.

Justin laughed outright and closed his computer. "Alright, no working today. You're right."

Kyrsten smiled then. She hugged him again before sitting at the table beside him.

"Anissa! How are you?"

Anissa rushed to hug Miss Emily, her small group leader. "Hi! I'm good. How are you?"

"I'm good. You ready for church?"

Anissa nodded vigorously. "Yes!!"

"Okay, well let's head into the classroom. Worship will start here soon."

Anissa was part of the third-grade group in the children's ministry of their church, where Anissa's family attended in Sylacauga. Miss Emily had been Anissa's small group leader for the past year.

After church, Anissa's parents came to pick her up, and she greeted them excitedly. She told them about all that she had learned and what fun she'd had that day. She could not wait to come back next week!

"Justin!" Madison whispered in her husband's ear.

Justin opened his eyes and turned to look at her. He raised an eyebrow questioningly.

"Look at Kyrsten," she pointed at their daughter.

Justin felt his breath catch in his throat when he saw their daughter. Kyrsten was standing with her eyes closed and both her hands lifted high as she sang the words to the worship song. She had never lifted her hands before.

He remembered when he had explained to her why people lifted their hands in church.

"Daddy, why are all those people raising their hands while they sing?" Kyrsten asked as she rested in her father's arms.

"It is a sign of surrender. They have given their lives to Jesus, and they lift their hands in surrender to Him. It is also a sign of receiving from God."

"Do people have to do it?"

"No, you only do it as a sign of love and respect, but don't do it because others do it. It has to be only for God."

Now, Kyrsten was the one with her hands lifted, and Justin knew she was doing it for God, not because others did it.

After worship was over, Justin sat back down and pulled Kyrsten into his lap. "You lifted your hands in worship," he said.

"Jesus saved me," Kyrsten shrugged. "Aren't we supposed to give Him everything?"

Justin nodded.

"You told me that lifted hands means surrender. So, I'm giving Him everything."

Justin hugged her tight, fighting the tears that built behind his eyes. Madison sat beside him and put her arms around them both.

Monday, May 25

Rawad signed in on the staff roster before heading back down the aisle. Before anything else, he wanted to check on one of the mares. She was going to have a foal soon, and though he missed riding her, he was excited to be able to take care of her and her baby when it came.

He entered the mare's stall, softly latching the door behind him. "Hey, how are y'all doing today?" He petted the mare gently. Then he grabbed his curry comb and started to groom her. The mare sighed with contentment. The movement of the curry comb on her back felt good.

Once finished with the mare, Rawad left the stall and went in search of Liam. They were supposed to clean a bunch of tack, and he sure wasn't getting stuck with the job alone.

"Mommy, look." Anissa held out a piece of paper to her mom.

"What's this?" Carrie took the paper.

Anissa giggled. "Read it!"

Carrie did as requested. It was a short story about their family. "When did you do this, Sweetheart?"

"They had us write short stories about our families on the last day of school."

"But that was almost two weeks ago."

Anissa shrugged. "I wanted to make it better. And our teacher told us that it would teach us more if we found out something cool about one of our family members and used that. That's why mine talks about pioneers. 'Cause Daddy's name means pioneer. I think they said it's Arab."

"Arabic," Carrie supplied. "This is very good Anissa. You need to show your daddy when he gets home. He will love it."

Anissa grinned. She took the paper from her mom and carried it back upstairs to her bedroom.

In her room, she sat on her bed with a stuffed horse. "I have the best Daddy in the whole world," she confided to the horse.

Chapter 03: Taken Away

Tuesday,
May 26, 2009

For I reckon that the sufferings of this present time are not worthy to be compared with the glory which shall be revealed in us. ~Romans 08:18

Completely focused, Rawad turned the horse around, and they completed the pole bending course a second time.

"Looking good," Liam called from the sidelines.

Rawad stopped the horse and faced his brother. "Shouldn't you be working?"

"You mean watching you train a new horse isn't part of my job?" Liam sounded hurt.

Rawad grinned. "Nope."

"Well, the way I see it, I should be paying attention when you train horses, so that I can pick up techniques for any horses that I train."

Rawad shook his head as he dismounted. He led the horse out of the open arena and they followed Liam back to the stable.

"Hey, how's that mare doing?" Liam asked.

"She's good. Once I get this boy put away, I'll go check on her. She may birth the foal yet tonight." They entered the stable.

Liam gave Rawad a knowing look. "Does Carrie know yet that you're probably pulling an all-nighter?"

Rawad shrugged trying not to look guilty. "I'll call her if I find out the foal is definitely coming tonight."

"There's no definite with these mares! Dude, you need to call her. Like, now."

Rawad led the horse with him to his empty stall and began to untack. "I'll call her once I get this horse taken care of."

"You better." Liam left to continue his work.

Rawad groomed the horse, and then carried his gear to the tack room. Once everything was put away, he grabbed his phone and dialed Carrie's number. "Hey, I may not make it home till either way late or very early in the morning. I have a mare who's about to birth her foal, and think that'll be tonight."

"But don't you have to help with all the trail riders tomorrow? I was going to bring Anissa," Carrie reminded him.

"Yeah. That's why I'm hoping this foal will get here sooner rather than later."

Carrie sighed. "Okay. I'll pray there's no complications with the birth and the foal's healthy. Hopefully, you'll be able to come home soon."

"Thanks, Carrie. I love you."

"I love you, too. Bye."

"Bye." Rawad put his phone in his pocket, and then went to check on the mare.

"Hey, Sweet Girl." Justin entered his daughter's room.

Kyrsten closed the children's book she had been reading. "Hi, Daddy!"

"How would you feel about going horseback riding tomorrow?"

Kyrsten's eyes lit up and she squealed excitedly. "Yes, oh yes!! Are we really going tomorrow?!"

"Yes, we are. Right after lunch."

Kyrsten hugged him hard. "Thank yoouuu!!!!!" She danced around the room.

Justin grinned. "You're welcome. Hey, you want to come downstairs? It's almost suppertime."

"Okay."

That night, while Madison put Kyrsten to bed, Justin grabbed his phone and stepped outside. He dialed his cousin's number.

"Hello?" Kathlyn answered on the second ring.

"Hey. I have an insane favor to ask of you." Kathlyn had been the only person he could think of that would be willing to help, if worse came to worst.

"Okay. What's up?"

Quickly, Justin explained the accusations that had been brought against him. "We haven't figured out how to prove my innocence. I let them check my bank account to prove that the money's not in there, but they keep saying I could have a different account overseas that I moved it to. Even though the money's not there now, they have transactions proving it was there. Plus, I was at work for all the times they wanted alibis for. They think I stole people's information from the DMV's records to hack into their bank accounts. They also think I stole other assets and framed some of our clients for it. I did not do it, Kathlyn."

"I believe you," Kathlyn spoke calmly. "How does this involve me?"

"If I can't prove my innocence soon, I'll be sent to prison. Madison and Kyrsten will be alone. And Madison currently doesn't have a job. We've been using funds we had set aside while I've been out of work. Would you be willing to keep an eye on Madison and Kyrsten? Help Madison find a job and just be a friend to them while I'm gone?" Justin rubbed his temples.

"I can. You realize I live in Shorter and run a stable? I can't come all the way to Sylacauga very often."

"I'm going to ask Madison to move to Shorter if I get taken away. She has no friends here anyway. I want her to have someone close by who I know will watch out for her and Kyrsten."

Kathlyn was silent a moment. "I will do what you ask. I will also be Praying for you and for your wife and daughter."

Justin breathed a sigh of relief. "Thank you, Kathlyn."

Wednesday, May 27

"Hey, Madison. Hold on a sec'."

Madison stopped in the kitchen doorway and turned to face her husband.

It was morning, and they had just finished breakfast. Justin had to talk to her before Kyrsten came back downstairs.

"I need to talk to you. Can we sit down?" Justin nodded toward their kitchen table.

"Sure." Madison sat down across from the seat Justin took.

"I'm sure you realize that if we don't prove my innocence soon, I'll be sent to prison."

Madison shook her head. "No, you won't be sent to prison. We'll prove your innocence!"

Justin held up a hand. "Hear me out. I talked to my cousin Kathlyn last night. If I get sent to prison, you'll be alone. You have no job and no friends nearby. Your family lives in Colorado, and my parents just moved to Texas. You won't have anyone to help you out. Kathlyn has agreed to keep an eye on y'all and help you get a job."

"I thought she lives in Shorter," Madison interjected.

"She does. I want you and Kyrsten to move to Shorter."

Madison was already shaking her head. "No. Should you get sent to prison, I will get a job here. Then, continue to figure out how to prove your innocence so you would be freed. But none of that will happen. You will not be sent to prison." Her voice firm, she said it as much to convince herself as him.

"Madison, please—"

Kyrsten raced into the room at that moment. "Daddy, look!"

"We'll discuss this later," Justin told Madison. He turned his attention to Kyrsten. As she showed him her newest drawing, he was aware of Madison getting up and leaving the room.

"Daddy!!" Anissa rushed through the small crowd to hug her dad. Carrie followed at a slightly slower pace.

"Hey, Sweet Girl!!" Rawad set down the bucket so he could pick up Anissa. After settling her on his right side, he picked up the bucket again with his free left hand. "Have you had a good day so far?"

"Yes!" Anissa nodded vigorously.

Carrie greeted Rawad with a smile. "I brought your lunch." She held up a brown paper sack.

"Thank you so much. I'll take it from you in just a moment. I need to put this bucket away. Y'all can come with me."

After he had put the bucket away, he asked Anissa, "You want to meet the new colt who came last night??"

"Yes!!" Anissa grinned excitedly.

"Alright!" Rawad headed to a box stall on the end of the second aisle, and Carrie followed. Once there, he set Anissa on the ground.

"I'll show you the colt; then I'll eat my lunch here. After I eat, I'll let my boss know y'all are here. I already have permission to take y'all with one of the groups I guide. He just wants to know which group y'all are going with."

"This is gonna be cool!!" Anissa could barely contain her excitement.

Carrie nodded and handed Rawad his lunch.

"Thanks." Rawad accepted the meal. "I'm going to let her meet the colt; then I'll eat."

"Hey! Who decided to have a party and not invite me?" Liam joked as he walked up to them.

"Uncle Liam!!" Anissa rushed to hug him.

"Hey there, Missa Anissa." Liam picked her up. "How have you been?"

Anissa rolled her eyes at the nickname. "I'm good. You know miss doesn't end in uh."

"It doesn't! Well, then it wouldn't rhyme with Anissa. Then what would we do?"

Anissa shrugged. "I like the other nickname better."

While Liam and Anissa talked, Rawad decided to go ahead and eat. He could show Anissa the colt in a minute.

Finally, Liam set Anissa down. Rawad finished his lunch, and then unlatched the stall door. "Alright, Anissa. You have to be very calm when you come in this stall," he told her, reaching out a hand.

She took his hand and followed him into the stall. "It's adorable!" she breathed.

The colt lay in a corner of the stall asleep. His dam, who had been dozing, lifted her head to check out the newcomers.

Rawad laid his hand on the mare's withers. "You can say hi to the colt. He's pretty social for a newborn. Most new foals keep to themselves."

Anissa knelt down in front of the colt. Awake now, the colt raised his small head to look at her.

"Hold out your hand to him, 'Nissa." Liam suggested. He and Carrie stood outside the stall door watching.

Anissa held out her hand to the colt, palm up. Eagerly, the colt sniffed her outstretched fingers. She giggled. Turning her hand over, she gently stroked his soft muzzle.

"Daddy, what's his name?"

"I don't believe he has a name, yet." Rawad knelt down beside her. "What would you name him?"

Anissa shrugged. "Is this the foal you helped last night? Mommy says you came home late 'cause of helping a horse have its baby."

"Well, I mostly just watched to make sure nothing went wrong."

"Hmm." She continued to pet the colt. Sighing contentedly, the colt laid his gray head on her knee. She giggled again.

Rawad grinned.

"Rawad?"

Rawad stood up. His boss, Cayden Norris, stood outside the stall near Carrie. Liam had left. "Yes, Sir?"

"The next group needs to head out in ten. You and Liam will lead it. I sent Liam to double-check that everyone has horses and required tack and gear. If your family's going, you need to hurry and get horses for them."

"Yes, Sir. I'm going to have Anissa ride double with me, but I'll get a horse out for Carrie."

His boss nodded and left.

"I'm sorry, Anissa, but we have to go, now," Rawad told his daughter.

"Okay." She stood up slowly. "Can we come back later?"

"Maybe." Rawad grinned.

Kyrsten could not contain her excitement. This was going to be so *fun*!!!

"Alright, Young Lady. May I help you mount?" One of the trail guides approached her with a kind smile.

Grinning, she nodded quickly.

Since she was not very tall yet, the man lifted her into the saddle. He then showed her how to put her feet in the stirrups. "What's your name?" the man asked her as he demonstrated how she must hold the reins.

"Kyrsten," she chirped.

"Well, Miss Kyrsten. My name is Liam. If you have any questions or trouble, just let me know."

"Okay." She nodded.

Another man exited the stable, leading two tacked-up horses. A lady and her daughter followed him. Kyrsten's eyes lit up. Hopefully, the girl would ride near her. Maybe Kyrsten would get a new friend!!

The lady mounted one of the horses. Then, after the man had mounted his horse, Liam lifted the girl up to him.

"Alright, we're going to head out on the trail, now," the man with the girl spoke up. "I will lead y'all while our other guide brings up the rear. If y'all have any questions or problems, just ask one of us. My name is Rawad, and our other guide is Liam."

Liam mounted his horse, and they started off.

To Kyrsten's delight, her family ended up near the front of the group. Sadly, she didn't get a chance to talk to the other girl, but the ride was fun anyway. The birds were singing in the trees above their heads. The air was warm; the sky was bright blue. Kyrsten loved watching the sunlight filter through the trees to make patterns of light on the ground. She could see the actual sun rays streaming down through the trees. It was so beautiful! *Thank You for riding and the trail and the pretty sun!!* Kyrsten's dad had taught her to thank God anytime she saw something beautiful or found something she appreciated.

Throughout the trip, their guides pointed out different animals and plants that they knew about. They were very helpful and cheerful. Kyrsten thought the ride was great fun. She especially liked the guide named Rawad. He helped everyone stay at ease and was always laughing and getting others to laugh. She wondered if the little girl was his daughter. They definitely looked alike.

"Alright, let's turn here, and we'll head back to the stable. A storm may be coming, and I don't want y'all to be caught in it," Rawad told them calmly.

Kyrsten looked up and noticed the dark clouds in the distance. "Daddy, is it going to rain?"

Justin replied, "Probably in a little while, but we'll get back before it starts."

He was right. They made it back to the stable before the rain. It was even still sunny over the stable.

When Liam helped her dismount, Kyrsten asked him, "Can I pet the horse before you put it away?"

Liam nodded. "I'll tie him up right here, and you can pet him."

Kyrsten beamed. "Thank you!!"

Liam smiled, and then left to help with the other horses.

"Daddy, can I go back to see the colt again?" Anissa asked after they had dismounted.

"As long as your mom is with you. I have to get these horses put up before I can go over there with you."

"Thank you!!" Anissa hugged him.

He hugged her close before getting back to work. Anissa raced over to Carrie. "Mom, let's go see the colt!!"

"Okay." Carrie smiled as her daughter raced ahead to the colt's stall.

"Daddy, don't you think horses are pretty?" Kyrsten was still petting the horse she had ridden.

"Sure, they are." Justin grinned. He and Madison stood watching her with the horse.

"Justin Levine?" An authoritative voice spoke behind him.

With a sick feeling in his gut, Justin turned to face two sheriff's deputies.

The first one spoke again. "Justin Levine, you are under arrest for fraud and identity theft."

Madison grabbed Justin's arm. "No, please!! You gave him a week! It's only been six days. Give us one more day!" she begged tearfully.

"Mommy, what's going on?" Kyrsten had stopped petting the horse to see what the commotion was about.

Madison ignored her daughter. "He's innocent, please!!"

"I'm sorry, Ma'am, but our orders are to bring him in."

In a daze, Justin allowed the second deputy to put the cuffs on his wrist. He could hear Madison's cries, Kyrsten's bewilderment, and the deputy explaining his rights, but he didn't know what to do.

"Time to go," one of the deputies told him.

"Please, let me hug my family," he finally found his voice.

Compassionately, the second deputy released one hand from the cuffs so Justin could hug his family goodbye.

Justin hugged and kissed Madison. "Promise me you'll go to Shorter. Trust Kathlyn. Promise me!" he whispered fiercely. He held his phone out to her.

"I promise," Madison managed to say. "I love you." She couldn't stop crying. She took the phone.

Justin knelt to hug Kyrsten. "I love you, Sweet Girl. Never forget that. Help Mommy, okay?"

"Don't go, Daddy!!" Kyrsten wailed.

"I would stay if I could. I'm sorry, Kyrsten."

The deputy recuffed his wrist.

"I love you both." Justin was struggling not to cry.

"Goodbye, Justin," Madison whispered.

The deputies led him to the car.

"Nooo!!!" Kyrsten screamed. "Daddy, don't leave me!!! Daddy!!!!" She tried to follow him, but Madison grabbed her arm and held her in place.

After the deputies had Justin inside the car, they glanced at each other. Their job had never been so hard.

After the sheriff's car was out of sight, Madison released her daughter. "Let's go home, Kyrsten." Madison didn't know what else to do.

"No!!" Kyrsten pulled away.

"Kyrsten, please—"

Kyrsten interrupted. "No! I want Daddy!!" She suddenly turned and ran off into the woods.

"Kyrsten!" Madison started to follow, but Rawad, who had witnessed the whole ordeal, stopped her.

"Liam and I will go after her. We don't need both of y'all lost in these woods."

Liam was already mounting. Rawad untied the horse Kyrsten had been petting since his horse was in the barn.

The brothers set off quickly to find the little girl. They needed to hurry. The storm clouds they had seen earlier were now directly overhead and the wind was picking up. They did *not* want to be caught in the rain.

Within a few minutes, they found her leaning against a tree and crying. It started to sprinkle, and a roll of thunder sounded.

Rawad dismounted. Liam sat on his horse close by ready to dismount if needed.

"Hey there," Rawad touched the girl's shoulder. "You ready to go back to your mom?"

The girl nodded and wiped tears from her eyes. "I want my Dad," she whispered.

"I'm sorry." Rawad didn't know what else to say. Gently, he led her to the waiting horse. He lifted her to the saddle before hopping on behind her. After getting her situated on the front of the saddle, he clucked to the horse.

They were almost out of the woods when lighting lit up the sky and thunder boomed.

The horse Rawad was riding reared in fright. Rawad gripped with his legs to keep from falling. He held the girl tightly. Just as suddenly, the horse dropped its feet back to the ground. Rawad breathed a sigh of relief.

"You okay?" Liam called to him.

"Yeah," Rawad managed to respond.

Not a minute after he had said it, the horse bucked as thunder sounded again. Rawad was unprepared, and he and Kyrsten were thrown off. Instinctively, Rawad tried to twist his body so the girl would not take as much impact. They landed hard and Rawad lost his hold on the girl. She landed beside him and lost consciousness.

The horse fled toward the stable.

Liam watched in horror as Rawad and the child were thrown to the ground. They landed with a sickening thud, and then lay unmoving.

Knowing he couldn't take both of them back to the stable safely, Liam urged his horse to a gallop. Once in the stable yard, he dismounted and rushed inside for help. He enlisted the help of a few workers before running to get Carrie and Anissa. One of the workers would get Kyrsten's mom.

In reality, Liam knew they should just bring Rawad and the girl back, and *then* get the family, but he felt that Carrie and Anissa should be alerted immediately.

He just hoped his brother was okay.

Chapter 04: Darkness

Wednesday,
May 27, 2009

Sylacauga, Alabama

O send out Thy light and Thy truth: let them lead me; let them bring me unto Thy holy hill, and to Thy tabernacles.
~Psalms 43:03

"Let's go see if your dad is done now," Carrie told Anissa.

"Okay." Anissa kissed the colt goodbye.

They left the box stall and started down the aisle.

Liam rushed towards them. "Come quickly!!" he gasped.

"What's going on??" Carrie was alarmed.

"It's Rawad. He got thrown."

"Daddy?" Anissa frowned.

Carrie grabbed Anissa's hand, and they rushed to follow Liam.

Everyone went to the site on foot since it was not far. It was also quicker that way than getting everyone mounted.

Liam, Carrie, and Anissa rushed straight to Rawad's side. "Rawad!" Liam touched his brother's shoulder.

"The girl," Rawad whispered.

"She's okay," Liam assured him.

"Daddy, are you okay?" Anissa asked fearfully.

Rawad's eyes stayed closed. "I love y'all. I love y'all." He breathed out a sigh.

Recognizing the sigh for what is was, Liam touched his brother again. "No! Rawad!! Wake up, please!!" He laid his head on Rawad's chest listening for a heartbeat. *Nothing.* "Rawad!" Liam started CPR as Carrie and Anissa watched. "God, please," Liam gasped.

"God, save my Daddy!" Anissa prayed aloud.

Finally, Liam sat back with tears pouring down his face. "He's gone."

"No!!!!" Anissa screamed.

One of the men touched Liam's shoulder. "Ambulance is on its way. Maybe they'll be able to do something."

Liam shook his head and stood up. "It's too late," he whispered.

Madison sat in the waiting room staring at the phone in her hands.

"You won't be sent to prison. We'll prove your innocence!"

"Promise me!"

"I promise."

"Daddy, don't leave me!!!"

Madison shook her head as if to shake away the voices. She looked at the phone she held. Justin's phone. She would keep her promise.

She pressed a side button on the phone, and the screen lit up. She quickly typed in his code. Madison felt tears build behind her eyes, when she saw a picture of her, Justin, and Kyrsten as his wallpaper.

Taking a deep breath, she clicked the contacts app. Scrolling to the K's, she easily found Kathlyn Shirah. She called that number.

"Hey, Justin! How's everything going?" a voice answered after only a couple rings.

Madison swallowed. "Is this Kathlyn?"

"Yes. Is this Madison?" Kathlyn sounded friendly.

"Yes. Justin asked me to call you if something happened. He was sent to prison late this afternoon. And Kyrsten got hurt, so we're at the hospital."

33

"I can't believe they actually sent him away," Kathlyn sounded sad. "Is Kyrsten okay?"

"I don't know yet."

"Well, I actually just finished work for the day. Why don't I pack a bag and head up there? I can help you out for a couple days." Kathlyn offered.

"You don't have to do that."

"Did Justin tell you about our agreement?"

"Yes, he wants me to move to Shorter. But that doesn't mean you have to come here. Don't you have a business?"

"Yes, I do. But I asked a friend to be ready to keep an eye on things just in case I needed to head to Sylacauga."

"Okay." Madison didn't know what else to say.

"I'll be there in a few hours."

"You could wait till morning; it's late."

"I'll be there in a few hours," Kathlyn repeated.

"Thank you," Madison spoke softly.

"See you soon." Kathlyn hung up.

"Madison Levine?" A nurse stood in the doorway of the waiting room.

Madison stood up, stuffing Justin's phone into her hoodie pocket.

"Follow me." The nurse nodded to her.

Madison followed the nurse down a couple different hallways before they arrived in front of a closed door.

The nurse opened the door to allow Madison entrance. She closed the door again once Madison was inside.

Madison immediately went to her daughter's bedside. "Kyrsten?"

"She's sleeping right now."

For the first time, Madison noticed the doctor standing on the other side of the bed. "Is she okay?" Madison asked anxiously.

"She has no broken bones and no internal bleeding. She does have a few scratches, but those will heal quickly. She has a minor gash on the back of her head where it struck a rock, but I stitched that up. It should be fine."

Madison breathed a sigh of relief.

With a compassionate look, the doctor continued. "There's more, and I'm afraid it's bad news," he said. "The impact to her head caused some damage. It's a miracle that's all there is. If she had landed even slightly differently, she could have been paralyzed. She might even have been killed. Yet, she is fully responsive and has complete use of her limbs."

"Wait, you didn't explain what the damage to her head is." Madison frowned.

"Your daughter might have trouble with her eyesight. Though, it is still possible she will be okay when the swelling goes down."

"You mean my daughter is blind?!" Madison was stunned.

"She might be. But we won't know until she awakens."

Kathlyn entered the hospital and headed straight to the receptionist desk. "I'm here to see Madison and Kyrsten Levine."

"Are you family?" the receptionist asked.

"Yes." Well, she was Justin's cousin at least.

"Kyrsten Levine is in room 162."

"Thank you." Kathlyn walked down the hallway until she found the right room. She knocked on the closed door.

"Come in," a female voice said softly.

Kathlyn stepped into the room, closing the door behind her. A young girl lay sleeping in the hospital bed, and a woman sat in a chair close to the bed. The woman was red-eyed as if she'd been crying. "My name is Kathlyn. You're Madison?"

The woman nodded. "And this is Kyrsten." She gestured to the little girl in the bed.

"What happened to her?" Kathlyn queried.

Madison quickly explained how the accident had occurred. "The doctor says she's going to have trouble with her eyesight. What if she's blind?" Fresh tears filled her eyes.

Kathlyn stepped closer. "I'm so sorry. I realize this is very hard for you. Does she know, yet?"

Madison shook her head. "She hasn't woken up, yet. The doctor says it'll be soon, though."

Kathlyn nodded. She grabbed an extra chair and brought it close to the bed. As she set it down, Kyrsten's eyelids flickered.

Madison leaned forward and grabbed her daughter's hand. "Kyrsten?" she whispered.

"Mommy?" the girl murmured. She opened her eyes, and blinked rapidly. "Mommy, where are you??!" She sounded frantic now. She tried to sit up.

Madison firmly pressed a hand against Kyrsten's shoulder to make her lie back down. "I'm right here, Kyrsten," she spoke calmly.

"Why are you blurry?" Kyrsten sounded confused.

"You will be fine. You hit your head in the fall. So, we just have to give your eyes some time to heal, okay?" Madison bit her lip.

Kyrsten did not respond.

Madison tried to think of what to do. She glanced at Kathlyn helplessly.

Kathlyn gently touched Kyrsten's right arm. "Hello, Sweet Girl. My name is Kathlyn. I'm your daddy's cousin, and I'd love to be your friend."

"Daddy's cousin?"

"Yes. How much can you see?"

"Everything is fuzzy."

Kathlyn spoke assuringly. "When you hit your head, it hurt your eyes. So, currently, you can't see very well, but that should heal with time. It'll take some adjustment, but you'll be okay, whether your eyes get better or not get better," Kathlyn explained carefully.

"Is Daddy coming back?" Kyrsten whispered. A single tear slid down her cheek.

"I don't know," Madison answered. She expected Kyrsten to cry and demand her dad come home, but the girl did neither. She lay there silent and still.

Kathlyn finally sat down in her chair. "Can I pray over you, Kyrsten?" she asked.

Kyrsten only nodded. She closed her eyes.

Kathlyn prayed aloud. She asked God to take care of Kyrsten emotionally and mentally. She asked that Kyrsten be healed and that God would use current circumstances to draw Kyrsten closer to Him.

After the prayer, everyone fell silent, and Kyrsten soon fell back asleep.

Madison finally spoke, "I didn't expect her to take it so well."

"She seems to be alot like Justin. Whenever he was given drastic life-changing news, he would get real quiet and keep his emotions inside. I don't know if he still does that."

"I believe he still does."

Kathlyn continued. "I'm worried that if that's what she's doing, it'll make it worse. Unless God works in her emotionally, she could have problems in the future. Does that make sense?"

Madison nodded. "I wish she had a friend she could talk to. She may not talk to me. That's one reason Justin wants us to move to Shorter. Neither of us has any friends here."

Sunday, May 31

"Hey, can I get you anything?" Kathlyn gently touched Madison's shoulder to rouse her.

Madison sat up straighter. "I'm sorry, I didn't mean to fall asleep."

Kathlyn chuckled. "You're not bothering me. I just figured you'd rather go to bed instead of sleeping in that chair."

Madison nodded. "I need to check on Kyrsten, again."

"I just checked on her. She's asleep. She's fine; you need to go to bed." Kathlyn knew Madison had barely slept for the past three days.

Madison got up and headed up the steps to her bedroom.

Kathlyn turned off all the lights before heading upstairs as well. She was staying in the guest room that was right across the hall from Kyrsten's bedroom.

Kyrsten had finally been released to come home from the hospital earlier that afternoon. The swelling in her head had gone down for the most part, but she was still having a little trouble with her vision.

Over the next few days, Kathlyn would help Madison pack up everything to be able to move to Shorter.

She hoped that Madison and Kyrsten would benefit from this transition.

Monday, June 01

"Anissa, can I get you anything to eat?"

"No." Anissa continued to stare out of the living room window.

They had gotten home after the funeral an hour ago. Anissa didn't want food. She just wanted her dad back. Anissa could hear her mom and Uncle Liam talking in low tones in the hallway. Probably about her. Or something else. Either way, Anissa didn't really care.

Uncle Liam entered the living room and knelt in front of her chair. "Nissa, can you look at me? Is there anything I can do for you?"

Anissa remained silent, looking out the window. Though she had been staring out the window for awhile, she wasn't actually seeing what was going on outside. She was just staring off into space.

"Anissa?" Uncle Liam persisted momentarily. Finally, with a sigh, he stood up. He turned to leave the room.

"There is something you can do for me."

Anissa's voice stopped Liam in his tracks. He turned back around to face her. "What's that?"

Anissa finally turned her head to look at him. "Tell me..." tears started to gather in her eyes. "Tell me how Daddy died."

"Okay." Liam sat down in a chair facing her. "There was a little girl who had gone on the trail ride with us. After we got back, her dad was taken away by the police. She was crying and ran into the woods. Rawad, your dad, and I mounted up and rode into the woods after her. You know that storm that we saw in the distance near the end of the trail ride?"

Anissa nodded. "It was raining when Daddy died," she whispered.

Liam continued. "Well, the storm started right when we found her. Your dad put her up on his horse, and we began to ride back. He was actually not riding his personal horse; he was riding a different one. Anyway, the horse got spooked by the storm. Your dad and the girl were thrown. By the time I got help, it was too late," Liam's voice was hushed now.

Anissa sat silently a moment. "Was the girl killed in the fall, too?"

Liam shrugged. "As far as I know, she survived. But she had to be rushed to the hospital."

"What was her name?"

"I don't know. All the riders were required to write down their names and information on a roster for the ride, so hers would be there."

"Next time you're at work, could you check for me?" Anissa requested quietly.

Liam nodded. "Sure."

Tuesday, June 02

Anissa wandered through the house searching for her mom. After a couple minutes, she found her in the kitchen. "Mom?"

Carrie looked up suddenly, surprised. "Hey. Do you need something?" She pushed her hair back behind her shoulder.

"I was looking for you. Are you okay?"

Carrie shrugged and pushed her hair back again.

Anissa remembered a few times when she had watched her dad figure out in a moment what might be bothering his wife. When Anissa had asked him about it, he'd said, "Your mother is not that hard to figure out. She has certain tells. Watch; you'll figure it out." Well, Anissa watched, but she was just beginning to understand. She knew now something was not right. She didn't know what exactly, but Carrie seemed stressed. She was standing with both hands flat on the countertop, but she wouldn't stay still. And she kept pushing her hair back, something she only did when stressed or overthinking. "Mom?"

Carrie sighed. "I need a job, Anissa. A good job that will support us both. But I also want to make sure I can still spend alot of time with you. I know you will be at the stable alot, but…" she let her words trail off.

Anissa crossed the room so she could hug her mom. "I love you."

"I love you too, Sweetheart."

Chapter 05: Legacy

Praise ye the LORD. Blessed is the man that feareth the LORD, that delighteth greatly in His commandments. His seed shall be mighty upon earth: the generation of the upright shall be blessed. Wealth and riches shall be in his house: and his righteousness endureth for ever. ~Psalms 112:01-03

Madison looked up at the sound of approaching footsteps. The twenty-minute wait had seemed forever long. But finally, he was outside the door.

Madison had finally made the almost three-hour drive from Sylacauga to the Holman Correctional Facility near Atmore, Alabama. She had to tell Justin what had happened.

The door across the room opened, and a guard allowed Justin to walk in and sit at the table facing her.

The guard left the holding room, closing the door behind him.

Madison so badly wanted to rush to hug Justin, but she told herself to remain seated.

"Hey, how are you?" Justin spoke first.

"Hi, I'm honestly not okay. I need you home, and Kyrsten…" her voice broke, and she couldn't continue.

"Have you talked to Kathlyn?"

Madison nodded. "She's at the house with Kyrsten right now."

"Good." Justin sighed. "Are y'all heading to Shorter soon?"

"We have to pack everything first."

Justin nodded once. "You'll need money, especially with fees and stuff from all of this. Kathlyn will help you find a house in Shorter. Just sell our house in Sylacauga, and when I get out, I'll come to Shorter."

"Are you sure?"

"Yes. I believe it'll be for the best."

"Okay."

"How is Kyrsten?" Justin inquired.

Madison took a deep breath. "Something happened after you were taken away. Kyrsten was crying and ran off into the woods. The trail guides went after her and found her. There was a storm coming, and one of the horse's spooked, they said. Kyrsten and the guide she was riding with were thrown. The guide died, and Kyrsten hit the back of her head."

"Is she okay?!" Justin demanded.

Madison blinked a few times. "She is having some trouble with her eyes, but the doctor says she should be fine here soon. There's just some swelling that needs to go down. The doctor says he wants me to bring her in after a few weeks just to check that it's healing okay."

"How is she handling it?" Justin spoke finally.

Madison shook her head. "I don't really know. She hardly talks anymore. She just stays in her room, doing nothing. And honestly? I haven't been the greatest mother the last few days. I've been struggling emotionally over everything that's happened the last few days— your arrest, Kyrsten getting hurt…" Madison let her voice trail off and took a moment to compose herself. "I've basically just let Kathlyn take care of her the last few days. Which, she said it was okay, but I still feel bad." Madison bit her lip.

Justin took a deep breath and let it out. "I'm sorry I'm not there to help. I am so thankful that Kathlyn is there, though. And don't feel too bad about letting Kathlyn take over for a couple days. She understands the need to take time and process. Also, Kathlyn's always been very wise and understanding. So, if you or Kyrsten end up trusting her enough to talk about what y'all are dealing with, I think she'd be able to help. And I can tell you for certain that she's already been praying for the both of y'all."

Madison smiled. "She's very kind. I like her. She has become a friend to Kyrsten."

"That's good. I'm hoping I'll be cleared here soon, but at least Kathlyn will be there until I am."

"Oh." Madison leaned forward. "I needed to come see you sooner than later, so I talked to the lawyer. He talked to the warden's office. They let me in because they thought the news of Kyrsten might possibly sway you to plead guilty."

Justin shook his head. "I'm not going to plead guilty."

"Justin! They'll reduce the sentence! If you don't plead guilty, they'll lock you up for twenty years!"

"I can't plead guilty! They'll put it on my record permanently. I didn't do it, Madison!! If I plead guilty, then the real guilty man walks with no worries of ever being found out! Plus, I'll be lying, Madison. I'm not a liar. I never have been, and I won't start now just because it means a lighter sentence." Justin's tone was full of determination, and his jaw was set.

Madison sighed, letting his words sink in. Then, she slowly nodded. "I respect your stand, Justin."

Anissa looked up at a knock on her bedroom door. "Come in," she spoke softly.

The door opened, and her Uncle Liam entered the room. "Hey, 'Nissa."

"Hi, Uncle Liam." Anissa still held the stuffed horse she'd been playing with. Her dad had given it to her when she was very small. It was a black horse she had named Wind.

"I found out that girl's name for you." Liam leaned against the doorjamb. "Her name is Kyrsten Levine."

"Kirsten," Anissa repeated.

"Yeah. But it's spelt differently than the norm. It's K-*y*-r-s-t-e-n."

"Okay." Anissa nodded. "Do you know where she lives."

Liam shook his head no. "Do you want me to check?"

Anissa nodded again.

"Hey, you think you could put some shoes on and come to the stable?" Liam requested.

Anissa vigorously shook her head no. "I don't want to go to the stable."

Liam straightened and walked closer to her. "Because of your dad?"

Anissa shrugged. *Why should she return to the place where her father had died?*

"Anissa, the hardest thing I have ever done was to go back to work on Monday, knowing my brother would not be there. It was like a punch in the gut to walk past his horse's stall and not see him there. To know I won't hear his voice again."

"What does a punch in the gut feel like?" Anissa asked the question quietly, but curiosity filled her tone.

Liam shook his head. "You don't want to know. All I'll tell you is this: it feels like you can't breathe."

Anissa was silent for a moment. "Does it still feel like that?"

"Kind of. But you know what? I've learned that even though it's hard, it's also good to go back to the place the person you lost loved to be. It's another way to remember them."

Carrie knocked on the open doorway. "Sorry to interrupt, but we're supposed to be at the stable in ten." Her face was pale, and she looked tired.

Anissa wondered, *Maybe her Mom didn't want to go to the stable either?*

At the stable, Anissa lagged behind her mom and Uncle Liam as they walked inside.

"Carrie, Anissa, good to see y'all!" Liam's boss, Cayden Norris, greeted them near the stable entrance. "Follow me, please." He led them down one of the aisles.

When they reached one of the stalls, Anissa recognized it immediately. This was the stall where the new colt had been born.

They stopped in front of the stall, and the boss turned to face them. Because of where he stood, Anissa could not see into the stall.

"Anissa?" Cayden beckoned her forward.

Obediently, Anissa stepped closer to him.

"Anissa, I know your dad let you meet the new colt." Cayden waited for her nod before he continued. "The colt's dam was his favorite mare. He put alot of time and effort into taking care of her. He always said that if her owners put her up for sale, he was ready to buy her. Well, the owners don't want to ever sell her, but they do not want to keep the colt. We received a letter from them yesterday. They want to give the colt to Rawad in return for his love and outstanding care of the mare."

Carrie inhaled softly.

"Because Rawad is no longer able to care for the colt or the mare, Liam will take over care of the mare. But he will not be caring for the colt."

Anissa frowned slightly.

"We are giving the colt to you, Anissa."

Anissa's eyes filled with tears. "W-hat?" she quavered.

"The colt will be entirely your responsibility. Liam will show you what to do and help you train the colt, but you are the one who must take care of him. And I'd say that your first task is coming up with a name for him." The boss smiled.

Anissa was at a loss for words.

"Anissa, I want you and Carrie to know that I and all of the staff deeply respected Rawad. He was an exemplary worker, and he always put everyone at ease. He knew what his priorities were, and he remained diligent and faithful for the entire time he was here. He was a good friend to all of us, and we will really miss him. If you or Carrie need anything, please let me know. I hope to see y'all around more while you take care of that colt. Oh, another thing. When the colt is about three years old, you can begin riding him. Again, Liam will help with training. If you need any riding lessons beforehand, I will enlist one of the instructors to teach you, free of charge. Consider it my way of thanking Rawad for all he did in his time here. It's also a way of ensuring you two stick around." Cayden grinned.

"Thank you," Carrie spoke softly.

Anissa faced her dad's boss. "His name is Rawad, and I want to train him the way my Dad would have."

Liam knelt beside her and put an arm around her shoulders. "Of course, we will train him your dad's way. I'll teach you what to do by letting you train while I instruct from the sidelines. That's how your dad taught me. And I think Rawad is the perfect name. Your colt will carry my brother's legacy with that name." Liam's voice dropped to a whisper with the last sentence.

They would all miss Rawad very much.

"Hey, 'Nissa? I checked the roster for the trail ride. The girl, Kyrsten's, address was on there. The funny thing is, she lives only a couple streets over from my house." Liam informed her as he entered the living room.

"So, she's not far from my house either?" Anissa raised an eyebrow.

"That is correct."

"Can you take me to her house?"

Liam looked up in surprise. "Why?!"

"Because, I feel like I need to talk to her."

"Why would you need to talk to her?" Carrie inquired with a small frown.

"Do you remember when Daddy wanted to buy Rawad's dam?"

Liam had to remind himself that the Rawad she spoke of was her colt, not her dad. "Yes?"

"He told me a story about it. He said that the people were selling some of their horses, so he asked to buy Rawad's dam. They said 'no'. He wasn't happy, and he went to see them to change their minds. He said the mare was the lady's grandma's favorite horse, and the grandma was sick. So, they had the grandma at their house. He said the horse was special to the grandma, so they wouldn't sell her. He said talking to them made him understand and made it better."

Carrie nodded. She remembered when all of that had happened.

"I want to meet the girl," Anissa insisted.

"Okay, when?" Liam agreed cautiously. He already knew, though, that he would do as she asked. She'd brought his older brother into it; how could he refuse?

"Can we go now?"

"Now?" Carrie voiced the question before Liam could.

Liam checked his watch. It was early afternoon, so the family would probably be at home. It was June, so the girl would not be in school.

"Yes, I want to go now," Anissa replied seriously.

"Okay then, let's hop in my truck. I'll take you." Liam stood up from his seat. "You coming, Carrie?"

"You sound like Rawad," Carrie whispered. She stood up.

Madison surveyed the neatly labeled boxes in the living room. It wouldn't be very long until they were ready to find a place in Shorter. She'd already listed their house in Sylacauga for sale. It was crazy how fast things were moving along.

A knock sounded on the door. "I'll get it," Kathlyn called from the hallway.

Kathlyn opened the door to three people standing nervously on the porch. "Hello?" she asked curiously.

"Hi, I'm Anissa. Is this where Kyrsten Levine lives?" Anissa had rehearsed that line on the way over.

Kathlyn raised an eyebrow. "Are you a friend of Kyrsten?"

Liam spoke up, "My name is Liam Ditka. I work at the stable nearby. My brother and I rode out to find Kyrsten in the woods not too long ago."

Kathlyn frowned. "You might as well come in. I'm Kathlyn Shirah."

"I'm Carrie Ditka," Carrie murmured as they entered the house.

Kathlyn directed them to the kitchen before retrieving Madison. "There's people here, the Ditkas. Do you know them?"

Madison shook her head and frowned. "No."

"Apparently the man and his brother are the ones who rode out after Kyrsten the night she hit her head." Madison followed Kathlyn to the kitchen. "Hello," she greeted. "I'm Madison Levine."

The Ditkas briefly introduced themselves.

"Is Kyrsten your daughter?" Anissa was curious.

"Yes, she is." Madison addressed Liam, "You rode after her, correct?"

Liam swallowed. "My brother and I did."

"Thank you. And please thank your brother for me."

"My Daddy is dead," Anissa informed Madison rather bluntly.

Madison eyes widened. "Is he the man who was thrown with my daughter?"

Carrie nodded.

"I am so sorry," Madison whispered. She leaned against the wall behind her. "So, the fall killed him?"

Liam grimaced. "He twisted to keep Kyrsten from taking the impact. They said that with how and where he hit the ground, it paralyzed and then killed him." He rubbed the back of his neck, fighting the images that rose in his mind. He could remember the entire incident in full-color detail.

Madison was overwhelmed. This man had died saving her daughter.

Kathlyn spoke up from her position near the doorway. "I don't know if this helps, but Kyrsten was rushed to the hospital afterward. I spoke to the doctor a couple days later, and he told me that he had been apprised of the entire scenario." She focused her gaze on Anissa. "He said if your dad had not protected her from the impact the way he did that she would have died. He saved her life doing what he did."

Carrie's eyes filled with tears. "I didn't know," she whispered.

Anissa looked up at Madison. "Can I meet your daughter?" she asked quietly.

Madison hesitated. "I would say 'yes', but I don't think she'll talk to you. She barely talks to me and Kathlyn. She lost her sight when they were thrown, and she's been quiet and uncooperative ever since."

"Let her try, Madison; it can't hurt," Kathlyn intervened.

Madison looked at Kathlyn with surprise. "Okay," she said after a few minutes.

"I'll take Anissa up alone so Kyrsten doesn't feel bombarded." Kathlyn beckoned for Anissa to follow her. They headed upstairs to Kyrsten's room, leaving Madison with Carrie and Liam in the kitchen.

Kathlyn knocked on Kyrsten's door briefly before entering. Anissa followed her cautiously.

"Mom?" Kyrsten questioned. She sat on her bed staring at nothing.

"No, it's Kathlyn. Your mom is downstairs."

"Oh."

"I brought someone with me. Her name is Anissa. I'll be here if you need me, but I'm going to let Anissa talk to you." Kathlyn nodded for Anissa to go ahead.

"Hi." Anissa slowly moved closer to the bed. "How old are you? I'm nine."

Kyrsten did not reply.

"How are you doing?" Anissa had no clue what else to say.

"Go away."

Anissa was taken aback. No one had ever said that to her before. She glanced briefly at Kathlyn; then returned her attention to Kyrsten. "What do you like to do?"

Her question was met with silence.

Anissa thought again of the story her dad had told her. After he talked to the mare's owners, they ended up becoming friends. And of course, they had tried to give him the colt who was now Anissa's. "I want to be friends," she told Kyrsten.

"Go away!! I don't want a friend! I can't see right, and I can't do anything! The only person I want is my Dad, but they took him away!!!" Kyrsten yelled suddenly. She fought the tears that began to threaten to fall.

Anissa stepped closer. "I lost my Dad, too. He died."

"I don't care!" Kyrsten declared.

Still standing in the doorway, Kathlyn wanted to intervene, but she didn't think it was wise.

"He died saving you!!" Anissa cried. A tear rolled down her cheek.

Now, she had caught Kyrsten's attention. "What?"

"My Daddy went to get you out of the woods. Y'all were thrown, and he twisted so he'd hit the ground first. He died." Anissa struggled to speak evenly.

"I'm sorry," Kyrsten whispered.

"I'm sorry you're having trouble seeing."

The girls were quiet for a moment.

"Where did your dad get taken?" Anissa asked tentatively.

"To prison, but he's not a bad guy." Kyrsten was quick to defend Justin.

"Okay," Anissa agreed without question. "Can we be friends??"

"Yes. But we're moving."

"Moving?" Anissa frowned.

Kyrsten just nodded.

"Well, we can be friends anyway." She grinned. "Where are you moving to?" Anissa couldn't leave it alone.

"To Shorter."

Chapter 06: Leaving Sylacauga

Sylacauga, Alabama

**Friday,
June 12, 2009**

Behold, I will do a new thing; now it shall spring forth; shall ye not know it? I will even make a way in the wilderness, and rivers in the desert. ~Isaiah 43:19

Kyrsten pressed her face against the cool glass of the window. She imagined what it must look like—Sylacauga and the life she had always known, slowly fading away.

She listened to the sound of their vehicle's engine. This vehicle would carry her all the way to Shorter, but she knew it couldn't take all of her. Her heart had been left behind in Sylacauga, along with her failing eyesight. She may never even know what her new home looked like, may never see it for herself. The doctor said her eyes would get better, but if so, shouldn't it have happened already?

Kyrsten thought about what her mom had told her. For a couple days, they would stay with Kathlyn until the purchase of their new house was finalized. Madison had sold their house in Sylacauga to a young couple. The couple was nice, but Kyrsten couldn't stop the resentment when she realized they were buying *her* home.

Kyrsten was also currently sorta mad at her mom. *Apparently,* her mom had gone to visit her dad at the prison *without* her. Who cared that he was not allowed alot of visitors while awaiting trial? She wanted her dad, and Madison should have taken her along. She wondered, *Did her Dad miss her as much as she missed him?* Surely, he did. She hoped he would come home soon.

Wednesday, August 05

"Hey, Anissa come here," Carrie called from her bedroom.

Today, Carrie was going through Rawad's stuff. This was her first chance to do it, since they were at the stable almost every day. Not only did they go so that Anissa could take care of and train her colt, but also because Carrie now worked there as well. After Rawad died, Carrie had accepted a job at the stable. She didn't get near as much money as Rawad used to, however. She was not qualified to train horses or teach lessons. She mostly did odd jobs around the place— mucking stalls, washing and filling buckets, cleaning tack, and grooming horses.

Anissa entered the room. "Did you need me?"

"I found some things you might want." Carrie patted a spot on the floor beside her. "I'm going through your dad's stuff."

Anissa seated herself in the spot her mother had indicated. She did not say anything, but she was curious.

Carrie handed Anissa several printed out pictures. "These are pictures of our family. I have copies of them, so you can keep those."

"Thank you." Anissa looked through the pictures. Some were of things she could well remember; others were taken when she was much younger. There were some pictures of the whole family and some of just Carrie and Anissa, Rawad and Carrie, or Rawad and Anissa. There was even one of Rawad by himself. She held that one longer, staring at her dad's face. *How she missed him!!*

"You can have these, too," Carrie's voice brought Anissa back to the present. She handed Anissa a couple small items of Rawad's.

Anissa looked over each one before setting them with the pictures. She looked back at the things Carrie still had in front of her. "Is that Dad's watch?"

Carrie nodded. She picked it up and handed it to her daughter.

Anissa examined the black outdoor-style watch. Her dad had always worn it. She could only remember a couple times he hadn't had it on. He always wore it face inward on his right wrist. He had been left-handed, so he'd worn it on his right wrist. Anissa was also left-handed.

"I thought he was wearing this the day he died," Anissa whispered, still holding the watch.

"Yes, but I got back all of his personal effects from the morgue."

"Can I have his watch??" Anissa requested slowly.

"Yes, you can."

Anissa hugged her mom. "Thanks."

"You're welcome. Are you going to wear it, or just keep it?"

"I want to wear it the way he did."

Carrie nodded in understanding. "Do you want help putting it on?"

Wordlessly, Anissa handed the watch to her mom and held out her right wrist.

Carrie wrapped the watch around Anissa's wrist, and fed the resin strap through the silver buckle. "Is this tight enough?"

Anissa nodded.

Carrie finished fastening the watch. "I remember to put it on, your dad would press his arm against his chest to hold it in place until he could get it strapped on."

Anissa had seen him do that. "I miss him. I wish he were still here," she whispered. A single tear escaped her left eye.

Carrie wrapped her arms around her daughter. "Me too." Tears filled her eyes. "I love you, Anissa. I'm proud of you."

"I love you, too."

Anissa checked her watch and sighed. Her mom said that once Uncle Liam arrived, they would all sit down and talk. The 'sit down and talk' part sounded ominous.

Anissa was 10 now. She had spent the last seven months missing her dad, going to school, and training her horse, Rawad. This month looked to be much the same as the last ones had been.

"Anissa?"

Anissa turned at the sound of her Mother's voice.

Carrie stood in her bedroom doorway. "Liam is here."

"K. I'll be in the living room shortly."

Carrie nodded and left.

Though she dreaded what the talk may hold, Anissa was glad Uncle Liam was here. He reminded her of her dad. He had actually offered several times to marry Carrie after Rawad died, but Carrie refused. She told him, "Liam, I appreciate your help, and I appreciate the offer. But I'm not going to marry just to make life easier. I miss Rawad, and I always will. But he's not coming back, and I have Anissa to think of. While, yes, marrying makes sense on the surface, it won't work for us. Anissa and I both love you and we really appreciate your presence in our lives. But I can't marry you. Anissa will resent you for taking Rawad's place, and I can't honestly say I wouldn't feel the same." Anissa agreed with her mom.

She made her way downstairs and to the living room. Inside, Carrie and Liam had already found seats. Anissa gave Uncle Liam a hug before also taking a seat.

"Okay, I need to talk to both of y'all," Carrie began hesitantly. "I am going to look harder for a different job. I know when I looked before, there was nothing, but I need to find something. The stable job is not providing enough for me and Anissa. Things were tight already when Rawad was still training, but now we don't have the training income. Plus, Rawad's funeral drained a good portion of our savings. I want to find a job that provides more, and one that would hopefully give me some days off to spend with Anissa. If I find another job, Liam, would you be okay with Anissa hanging out with you at the stable while I work? That way, she can continue training her colt."

Liam nodded. "That should work."

"What about days I have school?" Anissa questioned.

"You'll take a different bus after school that will drop you off at the stable."

Anissa understood what Carrie meant. "Okay."

"As soon as I'm off work, I will come pick you up at the stable, and we'll go home."

Anissa nodded.

"Just in case I find something sooner than later, I went ahead and told Cayden that I am looking for another job. I explained why, and he understood. He said he wants my two-weeks notice on his desk tomorrow, and if I keep working after that he'll consider it extra work days as a paid volunteer." Carrie explained.

Saturday, May 08

Anissa latched the stall door behind her and went to find Uncle Liam. She checked her watch as she walked. Her mom would arrive any minute. She had gone to a couple different job interviews, and would be back soon to take Anissa home.

"Hey, Anissa." Liam waved to her from the end of the aisle. Carrie stood with him.

Anissa walked toward them, noticing her Mother's wide smile. Apparently, at least one of the interviews had gone well.

"Anissa, I found a job! I start Monday," Carrie announced as soon as Anissa had reached them. "But, there's one problem."

"What's that?" Anissa raised an eyebrow.

"The job is in Montgomery, so I'll be further away." Carrie went on, "But, you can still spend the days I work here with Liam, and I will come straight here after work. I also will have more days off."

"Okay," Anissa said.

"So, am I losing you after all, Carrie?" Cayden had overheard the conversation and now approached them.

"Sorry, Cayden, but I need a better job for Anissa."

"I know, but I hate to lose you. I'll have to be sure to keep an eye on these two or they'll leave too," he gestured to Anissa and Liam.

Anissa grinned. "I don't plan on leaving ever."

"Good, let's keep it that way." Cayden high-fived the girl.

Wednesday, May 12

Kyrsten woke up in the middle of the night screaming. "Daddy!!"

"Kyrsten!!" Madison called her name.

"Mommy?" Kyrsten sat up. She was in her bed; it had been another nightmare. This was not the first time she'd had some dream about losing her dad, but this time it had been way worse.

Madison touched Kyrsten's shoulder. "You okay?"

Kyrsten heard something click. "I had a nightmare," she whispered. "I lost Daddy."

"Oh." Madison hugged her daughter close.

"Can you turn on the light? I don't like the dark."

"Kyrsten, I just turned your lamp on when I asked if you were okay."

Kyrsten began to panic. "I can't see you; everything is dark."

"Kyrsten, calm down. Give it a minute."

Kyrsten shook her head. "I can't see! Mommy, please, help me!" Hysteria threatened to choke her.

"It's okay; it's okay. Kyrsten, listen to me. I'm going to take you to the hospital. They'll make it better."

Tears streamed down Kyrsten's face. "Don't leave me," she demanded when she felt her mother pull away.

Madison pushed Kyrsten back against the pillows. "I have to get my phone; I'll be right back."

Madison rushed to her bedroom and grabbed her phone off the nightstand by her bed. She speed-dialed Kathlyn.

"Hello?" Kathlyn answered immediately. "Madison, what's wrong?"

Madison didn't know what to say. "I have to take Kyrsten to the hospital. Can you come?"

"On my way."

"Madison."

Madison jerked awake. She looked over at Kyrsten. Her daughter was sleeping in the hospital bed. She looked up at Kathlyn.

"The doctor wants to see you."

Madison stood slowly. She saw the doctor standing in the doorway. He motioned for her to come out in the hall. Kathlyn squeezed her shoulder reassuringly before allowing her to leave.

"You wanted to see me?" Madison asked once the door had closed and they were out in the hallway.

"Yes. I have the diagnosis for your daughter."

"Okay."

"Ma'am, your daughter is blind. Permanently."

Madison took a step back. "But we were told her eyes would get better." She felt her breath catch in her chest.

The doctor grimaced. "I'm sorry. There's nothing we can do. You're free to take her home when she wakes up." He left her standing in the hall.

Numbly, Madison reentered the hospital room.

Kathlyn looked up at her. "What is it?"

"The doctor says she's blind, and it may be permanent." Fresh tears filled her eyes.

Kyrsten stirred in the bed. "Mommy?" she whispered. "Mommy, where are you??!" she sounded frantic now. She tried to sit up.

Madison firmly pressed a hand against Kyrsten's shoulder to make her lie back down. "I'm right here, Kyrsten."

"I can't see you! Is it night?" Kyrsten sounded confused.

"Yes, it is nighttime." Madison bit her lip. How does someone tell her seven-year-old daughter that she may never see again??

"Then can you turn on the lights?" Kyrsten requested again.

Madison couldn't stop the tears that began to roll down her cheeks. "Kyrsten, I have to tell you something. The…" She took a breath.

"Mommy, please turn on the lights!"

Madison tried to think of what to do. She glanced at Kathlyn forlornly.

Kathlyn gently touched Kyrsten's right arm. "Hey. It's Kathlyn. Are you okay?"

"I can't see, because it's dark," the worried girl replied.

"Alright, anything else?"

"No."

"Well, that's good. As for the dark, I need to tell you something." Kathlyn glanced at Madison with a raised eyebrow. She mouthed silently, "Is this okay?"

Madison nodded for her to continue.

Kathlyn directed her attention back to Kyrsten. "The lights actually are on, but I want to explain why you can't tell."

Kyrsten frowned. "Is it something bad?"

"It doesn't have to be," Kathlyn said confidently. "The injury to your eyes has gotten a little worse. It'll take some adjustment, but you'll be okay, even if your eyes do not heal," Kathlyn explained carefully.

"So, I'm blind?" Kyrsten whispered. A single tear slid down her cheek.

"Yes," Madison answered.

Friday, May 14

"Justin!" Madison reached to hug him, but the guard holding him stopped her. "Please," she begged. "Let me hug him."

Sighing, the guard relented. After the hug, he grabbed Justin's arm and made him sit down at the table. Then he left the room.

Madison sat across from her husband.

"What's going on, Madison?"

Tears poured down Madison's face. "She's blind, Justin."

"What do you mean?"

"Kyrsten. She woke up screaming from a nightmare. I checked on her and we found out she couldn't see. She's blind."

Justin let out a breath and sat back, stunned.

"The doctor said it's permanent."

"Dear God," Justin covered his face with his hands.

"I don't know what to do," Madison whispered brokenly.

Chapter 07: Bold Stand

Monday,
June 28, 2010

*Say to them that are of a fearful heart, Be strong, fear not:
behold, your God will come with vengeance, even God with a
recompence; He will come and save you. ~Isaiah 35:04*

Kyrsten shuffled down the stairs with her right
hand trailing along the wall. When she reached the bottom
of the stairs, she tried to figure out which direction to go.
She had not really paid much attention when her mom
tried to explain where everything was in their new house.

"Kyrsten?"

She felt her Mother's arms wrap around her. "Good
morning, Mommy." Kyrsten hugged her mom back.

"You're up early." Madison commented softly. She
had not seen her daughter for very long when she got
home last night. The trial had run late, and by the time
Madison got home, it was almost time for Kyrsten to go to
bed. "Do you want to come to the kitchen with me?"
Madison asked.

Kyrsten nodded.

Madison gently led her daughter to the kitchen,
and helped her find a seat at the table.

"Did you see Daddy?"

Madison sat down across from her daughter. "Yes, I
did Sweetheart."

"Is he coming home soon??" Kyrsten asked
hopefully.

Madison took a deep breath. "Kyrsten, there is no
good way to say this. Your daddy was sentenced to eighteen
years in prison; he's not coming home."

Tears filled Kyrsten's sightless eyes. Her last hope
of having her dad back was gone.

"He will be staying at the prison in Atmore, so he won't be very far away. We'll be able to visit him some." Madison tried to reassure her daughter. She knew, though, that her words meant little currently. Yes, they would be able to visit, but that was not even close to having him at home. Madison understood at least some of what her daughter was feeling; it had been all she could do not to break down there in the courtroom when the sentence was read off.

Madison suddenly remembered something. "I have a letter for you, though. It's from your daddy."

"Really?" Kyrsten raised her head a bit.

"Yes. I'll go get that right now, shall I?" Madison left the kitchen.

Kathlyn entered the kitchen as Madison was exiting. "Good morning, Kyrsten." The words were both a greeting and a way to warn Kyrsten of Kathlyn's presence.

"Hi."

"Here you go, Kyrsten." Madison tapped Kyrsten's arm with the still sealed envelope.

Kyrsten did not take the envelope. "Can you read it to me?" She asked quietly.

"Oh, of course." Still holding the envelope, Madison sat back down at the table. She ripped open the envelope and pulled out a single sheet of paper.

"*To my lovely daughter, Kyrsten,*" she read. "*My sweet Daughter, if you are reading this letter, it means that I am being sent to prison for a very long time. I am so sorry to be leaving you and your mother. I did not commit the crime, but I do believe that God will use this time for His Glory. Try to be strong, my Daughter. Know that I love you very much and always will. I am Praying for you and your mother constantly. I miss you both very much. Do not be scared while I'm gone, dear Girl, but remember that we always have victory in Christ even when it feels we have lost. I will write again soon, Kyrsten. Love from, Daddy."*

"Mommy, I want to go to my room," Kyrsten stated only moments after her mother finished reading the letter.

"Sure, I'll take you there." Madison stood up and slowly led Kyrsten from the room.

When Madison came back, Kathlyn looked up. "I know I'm not Kyrsten's mother, but I have a suggestion for you."

Madison raised an eyebrow. "Okay?"

"Have you made Kyrsten figure out how to do anything by herself yet? I know she's blind, but she can still hear, feel, smell. She should learn to do things on her own."

"If you're talking about the letter, you know she cannot read at all."

"No, I would read aloud to her as well. That's not what I'm talking about. But she should be able to mostly get around the house without you leading her. And she can figure out how to open an envelope by herself. Even if she has trouble for awhile, you should at least make her try."

Madison only sighed.

"Has Kyrsten eaten breakfast this morning?"

"No. She wanted to go to her room. I will probably just bring her something later."

Kathlyn threw up her hands in exasperation. "That's exactly what I'm talking about, Madison! You do everything for her. She needs the responsibility of doing some things for herself."

Madison took an audible breath through her nose. "Okay, I know you're right, but I want to implement things slowly. She's blind, and her dad just went to prison."

He'd only been in his permanent cell for just over a day, and already boredom was about to drive him mad.

With a sigh, Justin let his head rest against the cot behind him. Currently, he was sitting on the floor leaning back against the frame of the cot. He drew his knees up to his chest and closed his eyes. Memories of years before flooded his mind, all the sweet moments with his wife and daughter in Sylacauga. He fought tears as the memories kept coming. He missed his family so much.

He wished he had his Bible with him. He had asked Madison to bring it whenever she next visited, but he had no idea when that visit would come.

Kyrsten sat in the middle of her bed playing with a baby doll.

She heard someone enter the room. Her mom or Kathlyn? Nope, neither. Her mom's stride was heavier, and Kathlyn was careful to warn Kyrsten of her presence. The person crept closer.

Kyrsten took a guess. "Hi, Anissa."

"Not fair! I was trying to sneak up on you!" Anissa sat on the bed with her friend.

Kyrsten grinned. "You'll have to be quieter for that."

"I was being quiet!"

"I could hear you easily."

"That's 'cause you're blind."

"What?" Kyrsten frowned.

"Mom says that people who are blind develop really keen hearing since they can't see. She said it gets to the point that it's practically impossible to sneak up on them. So, I decided I would try sneaking up on you before you reached that point, but I'm apparently too late."

"I have not really noticed until now, but I guess I can hear better now," Kyrsten said thoughtfully.

"Obviously." Anissa grinned.

"I got a letter from my Dad." Kyrsten changed the subject abruptly.

"Really?" Anissa sounded excited. "What did he say?"

"Basically, that he loves me and to be strong while he's gone."

"Strong how?"

"I think he means to be strong even though I miss him and even though I'm blind. You can read it if you want," Kyrsten offered.

"Where is it?" Anissa got off the bed.

"Mom said she put it on my dresser."

"Found it," Anissa said only seconds later. She came back to sit on the bed again.

"Since you're going to read it anyway, can you read it aloud?" Kyrsten requested softly.

"I guess it's hard not being able to read it yourself," Anissa sympathized. She unfolded the letter and read it aloud slowly. When she finished, she stared at it a moment. "I wish I had letters from my Dad," she spoke wistfully.

Kyrsten carefully scooted closer to her friend. She put her arms around Anissa and remained there wordlessly for several moments.

After a little bit, the girls parted and Anissa spoke, "Have you heard the stories of all the people who are blind, but it's not noticeable?"

Kyrsten shifted into a more comfortable position. "What do you mean 'it's not noticeable'?"

Anissa tried to explain. "I mean that they can do crazy things, work and communicate normally, and they're blind. But because of all the things they can do, people don't even realize they're blind."

"Do you think I might be like that one day?" For the first time, Kyrsten sounded hopeful.

Anissa hesitated. "Yes, but…" She needed to word this carefully. "Kathlyn says you're not trying to actually learn things for yourself; that you're just letting your mom do everything for you."

Kyrsten thought about this. "I guess that's true," she admitted. "But I'm scared to do things when I can't see."

"You won't know unless you try. I'll help you," Anissa offered, "and I know Kathlyn and even my Mom will help as well. And of course, your mom."

Kyrsten took a breath, and nodded. "You're right." She stayed silent a moment. "Can you help me with something right now?"

"What?"

"I don't know my way around the house."

"I do. I can show you where everything is." Anissa stood up.

Kyrsten stood up also.

Anissa grabbed her friend's hand. "As you may already know," she began in a very serious tone, "the room we are in currently is the bedroom belonging to my very best of friends, Kyrsten."

Kyrsten giggled. "Well, that friend doesn't even know where all her possessions are in that room."

Anissa stated confidently, "We shall fix that immediately."

As Anissa showed her how to find things, the girls kept giggling over her dramatic statements. Kyrsten knew she would not forget this day. She felt the first stirrings of hope within her. Maybe Anissa was right… Maybe it really would be okay.

Madison knocked on Kyrsten's door briefly before entering. She stopped in surprise in the doorway.

Not only was Kyrsten awake, she had obviously been awake awhile. Kyrsten was dressed with her hair brushed, and her bed was made. Currently, she was placing her neatly folded nightclothes in the dresser drawer.

"Kyrsten?"

Kyrsten turned around. "I thought I heard you knock. Can you tell me if my bed looks okay? I can't see it, but I remember how I made it when I could see."

"It looks great, Kyrsten." Madison came in and sat on the bed. "I did not expect you to be up already, today." Madison did not know how to express what she felt when she saw all that Kyrsten had done by herself.

"Mom, do you remember when Daddy got so excited that I raised my hands during worship in church?"

"Yes." Madison nodded automatically.

"Daddy told me that he was proud of me, and to always remember that God is my strength. In the letter he wrote me, Daddy told me to be strong. Anissa and I talked about how so many people can do amazing things when they're blind. I've decided to learn to do things for myself. Anissa helped me figure out how to get around the house and where everything is, yesterday. She said she'll continue helping, but I need you and Kathlyn as well…" Kyrsten ran out of words.

Madison reached for Kyrsten, pulling her daughter onto her lap. She wrapped her arms around Kyrsten. "Of course, we'll help you. Your daddy will be so proud of your decision; I know, I'm proud. I love you, Sweetheart.

Chapter 08: Tremble

Montgomery, Alabama   **Sunday,
July 04, 2010**

The LORD is my light and my salvation; whom shall I fear? the LORD is the strength of my life; of whom shall I be afraid? ~Psalms 27:01

"Kyrsten, oh my goodness!!" Anissa squealed at the sight of her friend.

"Anissa!" Kyrsten stood still in the crowd until Anissa reached her. She hugged Anissa.

"I can't believe you're here!! We have to sit together!" Anissa could not contain her excitement.

"Definitely!" Kyrsten agreed immediately.

"Anissa, is this Kyrsten?" Carrie appeared by her daughter's side.

"Hi." Kyrsten's soft answer was barely audible over the chatter of other people trying to find seats.

"Anissa," Carrie addressed her daughter, "You go sit with Kyrsten, and I'm going to sit with my coworker over there."

"Okay, Mom." Anissa's mom had invited a coworker to church with her. Because of that, they had come to the Montgomery campus of their church instead of Sylacauga. Carrie's coworker lived in Montgomery.

She sat down with Kyrsten to her right, Kathlyn and Madison on Kyrsten's right.

The first song was faster than standard worship, and all of the church's youth would jump or dance during the chorus. Anissa moved away from Kyrsten so as not to jostle her and joined in.

Kathlyn smiled to see Anissa jumping along with the other students during the faster song. She took DJ and Hilary to youth nights, but Anissa lived in another city, so she had never joined them. Obviously, she went to youth at the campus in Sylacauga.

After the first song was over, Kyrsten tapped Anissa to get her attention. She spoke in Anissa's ear, "I need your help."

"With what?"

"I need you to be my eyes. They should very quickly show the song name and artist at the bottom of the screen after each song. I need you to tell me what each one says. You already missed the first one, but I want the next two."

"Okay," Anissa agreed.

The next song was not near as fast, but Kyrsten liked the chorus.

> *I call Your Name*
> *And Your Love, it fills this place*
> *And I know, know, I'm not alone*
> *You're here*

The song finished, and Anissa leaned closer to Kyrsten. "'You're Here' by Highlands Worship."

"Thank you," Kyrsten replied. She started to say something else, but the next song caught her attention with the opening line. Kyrsten didn't try to sing; she just listened. The words awakened something in her spirit. A longing for the peace the song described.

Kyrsten felt tears fill her eyes when she heard the words of the chorus. She slowly opened her hands directly in front of her.

Anissa noticed the tears trickling down her friend's face. "Kyrsten?" Anissa spoke in her friend's ear.

Kyrsten did not respond.

When Anissa was about to tap Kyrsten's shoulder, Kathlyn waved to get Anissa's attention. "Leave her alone," she mouthed.

The song continued. The bridge spoke of the Power of Jesus' Name, the chorus spoke of the darkness trembling because of Him. Kyrsten focused on the meaning of each line, allowing the song to contain her full attention in that moment.

Okay God, Kyrsten prayed, *I know that Your Name is Powerful. At the sound of Your Name darkness trembles. Help me to trust You even though I don't understand. My life is Yours. I give You my Dad. I give You my eyes.*

The song ended, and Kyrsten immediately reached for Anissa. "The song," she whispered urgently.

"'Tremble' by Mosaic MSC. Are you okay?"

"More than okay."

After service, Carrie came back to the row to find her daughter. "Hey, Sweetheart. We need to head home. Uncle Liam is meeting us for lunch in Sylacauga."

"Okay." Anissa quickly hugged her friends goodbye. She and Carrie left.

Tuesday, July 6, 2010

Dear Daddy,

I miss you soo much!!! I hope you will be able to come home soon! I know Mommy told you I'm blind now. (Actually, my best friend is writing this for me. Her name is Anissa.) I recently heard a song that says that Jesus' Name makes darkness tremble. I know the song is right. I am doing my best to trust Him and be strong. I love you, Daddy, and I'm Praying for you.

~ Kyrsten

Justin's eyes filled with tears. He missed his little girl so much! But he was so thankful that she had friends to help her, and that she was trusting God.

He thought of all the times he had come home to music playing for Kyrsten. He was glad she had found a song to give her hope even though she was blind.

Thursday, July 08

It was barely light out when Anissa woke up on Thursday morning. She checked the time on her Daddy's watch. 5:02 am. She sighed and tried to go back to sleep. A few moments later, she rolled over and checked her watch again. 5:04 am. She groaned. She was tired, but she couldn't sleep.

She caught sight of her stuffed horse, Wind. Anissa pulled the horse to her chest and sat up. Caressing the horse's wavy mane, she allowed her mind to wander. She could remember everything in extreme detail.

"Daddy, can I go back to see the colt again?"

"As long as your mom is with you."

"Thank you!!" Anissa hugged him.

He hugged her close before getting back to work.

Anissa could remember how it felt when he hugged her. His hugs had always made her feel safe and treasured. That had been her last hug from him. That last hug had been her only goodbye.

Anissa took a deep breath. She had started crying without realizing it, and now, she couldn't stop. "Daddy, I love you, and I wish you were here," she whispered between shaky breaths. She buried her face in Wind's coat to muffle the sobs wracking her body. She couldn't stop. She had lost the most important person in the world to her. She wanted him to come back so badly.

But he wasn't coming back. He was gone from this world. Forever.

Friday, July 09

"Kyrsten? Your teacher is here." Madison entered her daughter's room. Do you want her to come up here, or do you want me to take you downstairs?"

Kyrsten shrugged. "Here, I guess." This would be her first official lesson with the teacher. Madison had started looking for one a few months ago at Kathlyn's insistence, but it had been hard to find a good one in their area. This lady had agreed to drive from Montgomery to teach Kyrsten at home.

In a few moments, Madison returned with the teacher. "This is my daughter, Kyrsten. I'll be downstairs if y'all need me." Madison left the room.

"Hello, Kyrsten. My name is Marlowe Bauguess; you may call me Marlowe. How are you, today?"

Kyrsten heard Marlowe Bauguess settle herself in the chair Madison had brought up earlier. She shrugged in response to Marlowe's question.

"So, here's how this will work. I will be coming each week on Monday, Wednesday, and Friday. At first, we'll work on basic stuff, and then progress to harder stuff later. I will be teaching you how to cope with the blindness, how to do most things for yourself, and we'll come up with a good way for your mother to homeschool you. Some of your sessions will be just you and me, and for others we'll include your mother."

Kyrsten nodded.

"Okay, so today we'll get to know each other a little; then I'll teach you how to count your steps around your bedroom."

So, the days went on. Kyrsten slowly learned how to cope with the blindness. She and her mother worked together to figure out ways to make things easier. Marlowe continued to tutor Kyrsten, doing much of the work orally. Every now and then, Kyrsten got to spend some time with her friend Anissa, great fun for them both.

Kathlyn helped Madison get a stay-at-home job that allowed her to keep odd hours so she could focus more on Kyrsten.

Anissa grew up dividing her time between school and the stable in Sylacauga. She matured and became more capable. She learned the values of hard work and diligence, and put them to good use. Every day after school, Anissa went to the stable to train her horse, Rawad, and to help her uncle. With Uncle Liam's help, Anissa trained Rawad to be a hardworking, yet gentle horse. She also took riding lessons. She became a very proficient rider, riding a strong and capable horse. Liam worked at the stable; Carrie worked in Montgomery. On off days, Carrie spent all her time with Anissa.

Part 02: The Lord's Battle

Chapter 09: Coming Change

*Friday,
April 29, 2016*

Be strong and of a good courage, fear not, nor be afraid of them: for the LORD thy God, He it is that doth go with thee; He will not fail thee, nor forsake thee. ~Deuteronomy 31:06

Justin had been surprised when he was taken out of his cell and brought to one of the closed visiting rooms.

He was even more surprised to learn that his visitor was one of the deputies who had arrested him after the trail ride with his family on that day so long ago.

"You wanted to see me?" Justin asked warily as the guard had him sit down.

The deputy waved for the guard to leave. Once the guard had left, closing the door behind him, the deputy spoke, "Yes. How are you?"

Justin eyed the deputy suspiciously. "What do you want?"

"I only came to talk to you." The deputy stopped with a grimace. "Let me start over. My name is Jordan Keith, and I would like to be your friend."

Justin did not know what to think of that.

"You have a family, right? I'm sure you miss them."

Justin looked away. The compassionate tone in the deputy's voice nearly did him in.

Jordan sighed. "Look, we can talk about whatever you want, but I really don't prefer the silent treatment."

"Deputy Keith, I don't know why you're here, but—"

"Jordan, just Jordan. At work, I'm Deputy Keith, but to my friends, I'm Jordan."

Justin just stared at him.

"I'll tell you why I'm here." Jordan leaned forward. "The hardest thing I have ever done was arresting you. I can still see the fear on your family's faces. I can still hear your wife declaring your innocence. Every time I see a child, in my head I see and hear your daughter trying to run after you, screaming for her daddy." Jordan tried to swallow back the emotion beginning to choke him. "And in the face of all that, you remained strong. You held your head high, and even though your heart was breaking, you still spoke courage over your family. How?"

Justin leaned forward as well. "Jesus."

Jordan blinked. "I should have known you would say that."

"Why is this affecting you so much, Jordan?" Justin asked quietly.

"I recently lost my family," he finally said.

"Are they dead or alive?"

"Alive. My wife left me a couple weeks ago, taking our baby girl with her."

"Are y'all divorced?"

"No. She just left, without a word. She had been acting a little strange, but she never said anything to me."

"Do you know where she went?"

Jordan shook his head evasively.

"I thought policemen can find that stuff pretty easily."

Jordan just shrugged. "I haven't looked."

Justin stared at him in disbelief. "You what? Are you crazy?"

Jordan had to grin a little. "Maybe."

"But why?"

"Doesn't matter."

"Yeah right."

"You know I could just get up and leave right now. Technically you are talking disrespectfully to a deputy of the law." Jordan's tone was mock serious.

Justin shook his head. "Nope. 'Cause to friends you're just Jordan, and friends have every right to tease each other."

Jordan gave a bark of laughter. "Is that so? Well, be that as it may, let's leave the discussion of my family alone for now." He shifted in his seat. "So, tell me. Your wife claimed your innocence. Want to tell me how you ended up here?"

Sylacauga, Alabama:
Monday, May 02

"You're working in Montgomery anyway. This way, you'll see Anissa a little sooner after getting off work each day. I double-checked, and Anissa can still hang out with me each day. She can even bring her horse. We can stable him there, and she'll still take care of and work with him each day. Plus, doesn't Anissa have a friend in Shorter? She doesn't have any friends here. She may even become friends with the stable owner. She was at the house when Anissa met Kyrsten."

With a slight frown, Anissa entered the kitchen. "What's going on? What are y'all talking about?" She didn't bother to hide the fact she had been eavesdropping.

Carrie sighed. "Liam got a job offer from the stable in Shorter, and he decided to accept it."

"So, he'll be working in Shorter?"

Liam spoke up, "Yes. You can still hangout with me. We'll have to trailer Rawad to Shorter. You might also get to see Kyrsten Levine more often."

Anissa had visited Kyrsten in Shorter only a few times. She would not mind the chance to see her more often. "Which stable is this?"

Liam chuckled. "There's only one in Shorter. Kathlyn Shirah owns it. Do you remember meeting her?"

"Sorta." Anissa shrugged.

"Well, you'll probably remember her when you see her again. I ran into her up at that horse show last week. She offered me a job, and I took it. Not much else there is to it."

"We'll figure out your schooling when we get closer to it," Carrie put in.

Anissa had already finished school for the year, so the thought had not even crossed her mind. "What about the stable here?"

"I love my job here, but I feel God prompting me to take Kathlyn's offer. Cayden is sad to lose us, but he even agreed that this might be for the best."

Anissa frowned. That couldn't be right. Her daddy had worked at that stable for years! Surely, they could not just leave it now?

They discussed the changes they would be making a little further before calling it a night. Liam hugged Carrie and Anissa goodbye before heading home. Anissa went upstairs to her room.

She looked at her watch. She had worn it for years now. She was 16 years old, and she still missed her dad like crazy. She may be getting older, but the love she held for her dad would never fade.

Now, apparently, Liam had decided to leave Cayden's stable, and Anissa and Rawad, her horse, must go with him. But she would never forget the stable here. Maybe when she was older, she would be able to get a job at the stable here… She wanted to work where her daddy had worked. Work with the people he had worked with.

With a sigh, Madison closed the lid of her laptop, glad to be done for the day. Her phone rang on the table beside the computer, and she quickly answered it. "Hello?"

"Mrs. Levine? This is Marlowe Bauguess. I am not going to make it over there today."

"Okay, is there another day that would work?"

"No. I'm very sorry. I cannot continue teaching Kyrsten."

Madison frowned. "Why is that?"

Marlowe's voice grew quieter, "My Mother just got diagnosed with dementia. I'm moving to Tennessee to take care of her."

"I'm sorry to hear that," Madison replied. "Thank you for letting me know."

"Goodbye, Mrs. Levine."

"Goodbye." Madison hung up, then stared at her phone for a moment. Now what? Marlowe had been tutoring Kyrsten for six years now. Madison did not know how to help her daughter homeschool since she was blind, nor did she have the time. Plus, Kyrsten still struggled to cope with the blindness, despite the years. Madison did not know how to help with that, did not have the knowledge and experience Marlowe did. And on top of all that, she was still trying to prove in her own way that Justin had been framed. Though, after six years, it was difficult not to just give up.

Still troubled, Madison stood up and set down her phone. Kyrsten needed to know that Marlowe was not coming back. Madison decided that since they did not follow traditional school anyway, then Kyrsten could have off for the summer early while they figured out how to school her without a proper tutor. Maybe Kathlyn would have some ideas.

Her phone rang again, speaking of Kathlyn. "Hey," Madison leaned against the wall nearby her.

"Hey, Madison! How are you? I have a question for you."

Did nothing ever dampen the woman's spirits? She was always excited about something. "What is the question?"

"How would you and Kyrsten like to come over tonight? I am hiring a new worker, Liam Ditka, and his niece will become one of my students, I believe. I invited them over so we could discuss particulars, and so I could become reacquainted with his niece and her mother."

Madison remembered Liam was one of the men to ride out after her daughter during that storm so long ago. "Sure, as long as Kyrsten feels up to it."

"Which means y'all are coming," Kathlyn stated confidently. "Just tell Kyrsten that Anissa Ditka will be there. Plus, she knows I'll just come drag her over if she thinks she wants to stay home," she was only half-joking.

Madison chuckled. "You are one determined woman."

"I'll take that as a compliment," she responded brightly. "See y'all later!"

Sylacauga, Alabama:
Anissa was brushing Rawad when her uncle found her.

"Hey, Kathlyn has invited us out there to see her facilities. We'll eat dinner with her while we discuss details of my job and yours too. We need to leave here in ten."

"Okay." Anissa did not like that her uncle had accepted the job in Shorter, but she guessed she at least would be able to see Kyrsten more.

A little over an hour and a half later, they had arrived at Kathlyn's stable.

Kathlyn carried them on a quick tour, even pointing out three stalls beside each other which they would use for Rawad and for Liam's horse, Hawk. There was also a stall for Liam's second horse, much to Anissa's relief. The second horse was actually her daddy's horse, Zane. Liam had kept the horse after his brother died, although Anissa shared responsibility for him.

After the tour of the stables, which was smaller than the one in Sylacauga, they headed over to Kathlyn's house for dinner.

They had only been at Kathlyn's house a few minutes when a knock sounded on the front door.

"Anissa, would you please get that for me?" Kathlyn requested.

Wordlessly, Anissa walked to the door. It felt weird since this wasn't her house. She opened the door, and her nerves immediately were replaced by excitement at the sight that greeted her. It was Kyrsten and her mother! "Kyrsten!!" Anissa drew her friend into a hug.

"Anissa!" Kyrsten smiled.

"I didn't know you were coming!" Anissa moved aside so they could enter.

Madison gently guided her daughter inside with a hand on her shoulder. "Kathlyn thought y'all girls might like to spend some time together."

"Definitely!" Anissa affirmed as Kyrsten nodded in agreement.

Surprisingly, Anissa was actually a little sad to be going home later that evening. She'd had fun at Kathlyn's house. She and Uncle Liam had a clearer idea of what to expect when they started at the stable next week. Madison had invited Anissa to spend her afternoons with Kyrsten until Carrie got off work. That was the best part really, hanging out with Kyrsten each day. Otherwise, Anissa still wanted to stay at Cayden's stable in Sylacauga.

Thursday, May 05

"Kathlyn?"

Kathlyn suddenly realized she had zoned out. She inwardly cringed. That was exactly what she told her students *not* to do. And now guess who had caught her!

"Yes, DJ?"

DJ grinned. "Where were you?"

"I don't think I have ever seen you mess up before, Kathlyn. That's almost unthinkable," Hilary commented as she rode Hara in lazy circles.

"Not entirely unthinkable; I am human after all," Kathlyn managed to reply.

"I said *almost*." Now Hilary was also grinning.

"I'm sorry, Girls. Let's end the lesson there. Y'all go untack; then meet me in my office."

Both girls dismounted and filed out the gate with Kathlyn following.

"Are you okay?" DJ asked sincerely.

"Put the horses away; then we'll talk." Face burning, Kathlyn left for her office. Inside, she sat behind her desk and took a deep breath. That could not happen again.

Almost fifteen minutes later, DJ and Hilary entered the office together.

"Have a seat, Girls," Kathlyn offered.

Both girls did so before looking at her expectantly.

"I want to apologize for zoning out like that. I know better, and I realize that it could have led to serious trouble. I am sorry, and it won't happen again."

"Of course we forgive you." They smiled at her.

"I know I've made the same mistake," this from DJ.

Hilary asked, "Do you know what caused you to zone out like that?"

Kathlyn nodded. "I am trying to figure out how to help two more girls. One is going to start at the stable this coming week with the same arrangement y'all have. The other is my cousin's daughter. Both girls have some major pain they're dealing with, and both girls refuse to let anyone in. Well, other than each other; they're best friends."

"Where do they live?" Hilary was curious.

"One lives in Sylacauga, the other in Shorter. Anissa Ditka and Kyrsten Levine. Kyrsten actually moved here from Sylacauga a few years ago."

DJ well remembered her own move from New Jersey. "We'll help," she spoke confidently. She looked to Hilary who nodded in the affirmative.

Kathlyn laughed. "I appreciate that, Girls."

Chapter 10: Friends In Shorter

Shorter, Alabama

Wednesday,
May 25, 2016

That ye would walk worthy of God, Who hath called you unto His kingdom and glory. ~01 Thessalonians 02:12

"Riders up!"

Anissa swung into her saddle, and checked her watch: 6:00 am. She watched Kathlyn Shirah ride to the front of the group.

"Forward!" Kathlyn yelled. Her Morgan tossed his head as they started off.

Per Kathlyn's invite, Anissa had joined eleven other teenagers on a riding trip to Sylacauga. Kathlyn had told her it would take them two days to get to Sylacauga.

Anissa was glad they were going to Sylacauga. She'd been in Shorter every day for the past couple weeks. She split her days by spending mornings at the stable with Uncle Liam and afternoons at Kyrsten's house.

The travel was slow, and Anissa found herself wishing for a friend to talk to. Her dad would have loved doing this riding trip. She shook away the thought, and patted Rawad's sweaty neck. It was very hot, and she and the horse were both sweating. No wonder Kathlyn kept reminding the teenagers to keep themselves and their horses hydrated.

Thursday, May 26

On the second day of travel, Anissa felt her excitement building. She started recognizing various landmarks that indicated how close they were getting to Sylacauga. How close she was to home. No matter how much time she spent in Shorter, Sylacauga was still home; it always would be.

Taking a deep breath, Anissa started walking towards the girl. The riders had arrived at their campsite in Sylacauga a couple hours ago. Anissa had been spared the duty of cooking supper, and she was determined to make a friend while she had time.

There was a girl sitting in the grass nearby, and Anissa approached her. She sat down beside the girl who had straight brown hair and light brown eyes. The girl was very skinny, which made her look tall. Though, Anissa figured her height was actually average for a teenage girl.

Pushing her hair behind her shoulder, Anissa started the conversation. "Hi. My name is Anissa. What's yours?" She smiled readily.

The girl responded easily. "I'm DJ. You new?"

Anissa nodded. "Yep. I started training under Kathlyn last week. How long have you been with Kathlyn?" Okay, so she had worded that question weird. *With Kathlyn?* She should have said under or something like that.

The girl, DJ, seemed to consider the question. "About eight months. Feels like forever."

"Are you from Shorter?" Maybe this girl lived near Kyrsten.

DJ shook her head. "No. I moved to Shorter September of last year. I used to live in Paterson, New Jersey."

"I've never been to New Jersey," Anissa commented thoughtfully. "I was actually born here in Sylacauga. My Mom used to work here, but wasn't getting enough to support us, so she found a better job in Montgomery. On the way to work, she drops me off in Shorter with my friend. I think I'll actually be going to school in Shorter next year." Maybe she was talking too much?

"Can you not stay home with your dad? Or does he work too?" DJ queried.

Anissa grimaced. "My Dad's dead."

"Oh no! I'm soo sorry!" DJ immediately changed the subject. "So, does your friend come to the stable, too?"

"Nope. She's terrified of horses." Anissa grinned. "My Uncle works at Kathlyn's stable though. I work in the mornings, and spend time with him; then I spend the afternoons with my friend. But when school starts up again, I'll have to work in the afternoons."

DJ nodded in understanding. "I work in the afternoons, and so does my best friend Hilary. We go to the high school in Tuskegee."

"Is Hilary here?" Anissa glanced around.

"Nope. She's… sick." DJ grimaced.

"I'm sorry!"

Their conversation ended abruptly because someone called out, "Supper's ready, Y'all!"

Saturday, May 28

The next morning after their breakfast, Kathlyn led the group of teenagers in a prayer for the day. Once, finished, she sent the riders to tack up.

Anissa tacked up Rawad slowly. She mounted and urged him to a walk. By her direction, Rawad walked over to where DJ was mounting her horse. "Mind if I hang with you, today?" Anissa asked as she stopped Rawad beside DJ's mount.

"Sure! I don't mind," DJ's tone was welcoming.

"What's your horse's name?" Anissa wanted to know.

"Sunshine. Yours?"

When Anissa patted him, Rawad arched his neck beneath her touch. "Rawad. He's a sliver dappled Gypsy Vanner."

"That's cool! I've never heard the name Rawad before." DJ seemed genuinely interested.

Every rider urged their horses forward when Kathlyn called out, "Alright, let's go!"

As if their conversation had not been interrupted, Anissa responded, "Rawad is Arabic for pioneer. What breed is your horse?"

"Palomino. Your horse's name is interesting! My friend's horse is named Hara; I don't know what it means. She's a Dapple Grey."

Anissa couldn't help asking, "Your friend or the horse?"

Though she glared furiously, DJ was grinning. "The horse, obviously!"

Anissa laughed. "Yeah, Dapple Greys are really pretty horses." Carefully, she changed the subject, "You said your friend is sick. Do y'all know what's wrong?"

As her smile faded, DJ replied, "She has iron-deficiency anemia. There's also some other problem that makes it where she can't absorb iron; her body rejects it. She's been completely unconscious for weeks, and they said if something doesn't change soon, she won't live."

"Oh wow, that's terrible," Anissa lamented. That would be hard to deal with, she was sure.

DJ visibly straightened. She spoke in a firm tone, "But God's going to heal her. I believe He will. He has to."

"You're right, of course." With a grin, Anissa said it lightly.

"You're a Christian, too?"

"Sorta." Anissa shrugged off the question. "Is your friend a Christian?"

"Hilary got Saved four or five months ago."

"Oh, wow! Her Faith is new! That's crazy!"

DJ shrugged.

"My friend is a very strong Christian. Stronger than me," Anissa commented.

"The one in Shorter?"

Anissa nodded. "Her name is Kyrsten. I doubt you've met her. She stays at home and does homeschool."

"My Mom doesn't have time for homeschool."

"Neither does hers, not really."

"Why can't she go to school with you?"

Anissa only shrugged. That was not DJ's concern.

Sunday, May 29

Anissa was excited to learn they were going to an early service at her church Sunday morning. Once they arrived, the teenagers were given ten minutes to use the bathroom before they were to meet Kathlyn in the auditorium.

Instead of going to the bathroom, Anissa spent the time talking to people she knew. When she finally checked her watch, it had been more than ten minutes.

She rushed into the auditorium and found a seat with the rest of the group.

Kathlyn scolded her, "Where were you? I was about to come looking for you!"

"Sorry! I forgot how many people I know here."

"Keep a better eye on your watch, next time," Kathlyn warned.

With a nod, Anissa whispered back, "Yes, Ma'am." They stood for worship.

Wednesday, June 01

It was Tuesday, and the riding group had made it back to Shorter. They had found several serve opportunities during their time in Sylacauga. After the hard travel, serve projects, and camping every night, all of the teenagers were exhausted.

Riding back to Shorter, Anissa had kept up a steady conversation with DJ to keep away the sadness. Sadness that she was leaving Sylacauga once again. Even though she and Carrie technically still lived in Sylacauga, they were there so little. Anissa missed it.

"Hey, how'd the trip go?" Liam asked from his place just outside of Rawad's stall.

Anissa startled. "How long have you been there?"

Uncle Liam grinned. "Answer my question, and maybe I'll answer yours."

Anissa turned back to face Rawad. She stared at the horse, trying not to cry. Uncle Liam's statement sounded like something her dad would have said. "The trip was good," she finally managed.

Liam nodded. "I've been here for about five minutes." Both were silent a moment before he asked, "Did Kathlyn tell you about the show coming in June?"

"Yep." Anissa finished grooming Rawad.

"You entering?"

"Probably." Anissa shrugged.

"You should."

Friday, June 10

"Next is number 20, Anissa Ditka, riding Rawad."

Excitement shot through Anissa when her name was called. This was her first ever riding show. She had done pretty well so far; this would be her last class.

She urged Rawad to a walk, and they entered the ring. The starting signal was given, and they began the jumping course. She completed the course with only one fault, which was very good for her first show. She rubbed Rawad's neck.

When she exited the ring, she caught sight of DJ and Sunshine waiting for their turn. She rode Rawad over to them. "Hi, DJ!"

"Hey! Oh! Hilary," she gestured to the girl sitting on a horse beside her, "this is Anissa. And her horse is named Rawad. Anissa, this is my friend Hilary. She regained consciousness this past Saturday." DJ finished the introduction.

Anissa remembered DJ telling of her friend who was sick and unconscious. "The sumac fixed her iron levels?" Though she had her gaze focused on Hilary, the question was directed at DJ. A Native American man in Sylacauga had given DJ sumac when he realized the situation with Hilary.

With a shake of her head, Hilary spoke up, "The sumac may have helped, but that's not why I'm awake. God Healed me; He woke me up. This whole week, I've been working and riding as if nothing ever happened. Only God can heal someone with no lasting effects. God healed me. He is my hope."

Anissa chose to ignore Hilary's assertion. "What's your horse's name? DJ told me, but I'm not sure I remember it."

"Hara."

"Cool. What does it mean? Or do you know?"

"It means joy, seize, or princess."

"Hmm. Interesting. Rawad means pioneer."

The loudspeaker crackled, "Number 24, DJ Devins, riding Sunshine."

"See y'all in a few." DJ and Sunshine started for the ring.

Anissa, as well as Hilary, remained silent while they observed DJ's ride.

Once her ride was finished, DJ rejoined her two friends. She had ridden well, but it was up to the judges to decide whether she placed.

Anissa smiled as she and Hilary praised DJ's ride.

The announcer called, "Number 25, Hilary Seawright, riding Hara."

"Go, Hilary!" DJ cheered. "You got it!"

Anissa smiled again. Hilary reminded her of a bolder version of Kyrsten. Anissa also realized, as she watched Hilary's ride, that she could learn a few things from this girl. She rode very well.

Once Hilary's ride was finished and she had exited the ring, Anissa and DJ congratulated her.

Very soon, the announcer called for the whole class to reenter the ring to receive their placement ribbons. The ribbons were given out from lowest rank to highest.

Finally, the judge said, "Number 20, seventh place."

Anissa felt a smile spread across her face as the seventh-place ribbon was affixed on Rawad. She patted her horse's neck.

"Go, Anissa!" DJ cheered.

She really had friends; Anissa was so glad.

Chapter 11: Future Good

Shorter, Alabama   *Monday,*
June 27, 2016

He that handleth a matter wisely shall find good: and whoso trusteth in the LORD, happy is he. ~Proverbs 16:20

Laughter filled the air over one of the wire-covered bridges in Shorter. "This is so fun!" Hilary cried joyfully.

Earlier that same month, DJ and Hilary had decided to ride their bikes across this bridge. DJ had done this multiple times before when she lived in New Jersey. Hilary, however, had never done it.

Together, the girls reached the end of the bridge and stopped their bikes.

DJ leaned on her handlebars. "Now, you know why I went out of my way to cross bridges like this in New Jersey!"

Hilary nodded. "Too bad there's not another bridge that's on our way to the stable."

"Speaking of the stable, we'll be late if we don't get going." DJ turned her bike around. "Come on, we'll ride across once more and head straight to the stable once we reach the end."

Grinning, Hilary followed her friend.

At the stable, Hilary and DJ signed in on the roster before setting to work on their chores.

"Oh, I'm sorry!" Hilary said when she bumped into someone.

"No worries." The man smiled. "I've seen you around, but I do not actually know you. I'm Liam."

"I'm Hilary, and this is DJ." Hilary gestured to her friend standing beside her. The two girls had been on their way to the tack room.

"Uncle Liam, where did you put Zane's blanket?" Anissa appeared at Liam's side. She immediately noticed Hilary and DJ. "Oh, hello. I see y'all've met my Uncle Liam."

"I thought you weren't working afternoons until school starts?" DJ queried.

Anissa shrugged off the question.

"Anissa!" Kathlyn walked up, leading another girl by the hand. "I have a meeting in a few minutes. Can Kyrsten hangout with you for a little bit?"

"Of course," Anissa readily agreed.

"Liam, they're delivering more shavings in twenty minutes. Can you handle it, please?"

"Sure thing." Liam headed off down the aisle.

"Thank you," Kathlyn called after him. She turned back to Kyrsten and Anissa. "I'll be in my office if y'all absolutely need me, Girls." She left.

Anissa placed a hand on Kyrsten's shoulder. "Kyrsten, these are the friends I told you about: DJ and Hilary." She made the introduction immediately so Kyrsten would be aware of the other two girls' presence.

"Nice to meet you, Kyrsten," DJ greeted warmly. "Anissa has told me about you."

"Hi," Kyrsten replied quietly.

"Well, I need to get back to work," Anissa said. Clasping Kyrsten's hand, she slowly walked away.

"I thought she told me Kyrsten is afraid of horses," DJ commented thoughtfully.

Hilary shrugged.

What they didn't know was that Kyrsten was not there of her own choice. Madison had gone to a meeting with her boss, leaving Kyrsten in Kathlyn's care.

A little while later, Kathlyn came back, having finished her meeting.

Kyrsten startled when Kathlyn touched her shoulder.

"I'm sorry, Kyrsten. I should have said something so you knew I was here," Kathlyn apologized.

"Don't worry, Kyrsten; you are not the first person to be scared by Kathlyn. She's very good at sneaking up on people," Anissa spoke in an assuring tone.

DJ and Hilary glanced at each other in confusion. The four girls were gathered in the tack room, after having finished chores. When Kathlyn walked in, she'd been in Kyrsten's direct line of sight; so why would Kathlyn have to warn of her presence?

A few minutes later, Kathlyn and Kyrsten left to head back to Kathlyn's office.

"I need to have a little discussion with y'all," Anissa said firmly once Kathlyn and Kyrsten were gone.

DJ raised an eyebrow. "Okay?"

"This is not to be repeated. But y'all need to understand a few things, especially if y'all are going to be around Kyrsten. One: Kyrsten is terrified of horses, and two: Kyrsten is blind. But don't talk about any of that. If she says something, then it's okay to talk about; otherwise, stay quiet." With that, Anissa left the room.

"That was intense," Hilary said under her breath.

"She's defensive of her friend. Plus, at least it answers our question about Kathlyn scaring her."

Hilary nodded.

After her discussion with DJ and Hilary, Anissa went in search of her uncle. She knew she had been slightly abrupt and short with her two new friends, but she was protective of Kyrsten. And she did not want the other girls to be completely oblivious to the situation. That would be unfair.

"Uncle Liam?" She stopped in front of Hawk's stall.

Her uncle was inside the stall grooming his horse. "Hey, 'Nissa. What's up?"

"Do you have time to do a training session with me and Rawad today? We've done the last several on our own."

"I believe Kathlyn wants you to join her classes with the other girls."

"I work mornings and spend my afternoons with Kyrsten. Those classes are in the afternoon."

"Kathlyn teaches classes any time of day so long as it's on the schedule. Plus, you really should go ahead and switch to afternoons. That way there won't be a huge routine shift just as school starts."

Anissa scowled. "School doesn't start for two months. I have plenty of time, and I don't care about a routine shift."

"Why is this a problem? It's not going to change how much time you spend with me, Rawad, or Kyrsten," he pointed out.

"No, but I like mornings, and I do not want to join Kathlyn's classes. You have been training me and Rawad for the last six years; I see no point in changing trainers now."

"But I'm not a trainer here, Anissa." Liam finished grooming Hawk and turned to face his niece.

"Why not?"

"Because Kathlyn's not going to put me in leadership over students until she knows how I handle myself in the training arena."

"You're the best trainer there is!" Anissa crossed her arms in frustration.

Liam chuckled. "I appreciate your confidence in me. But Kathlyn's terms are perfectly reasonable, and in her position, I would do the same."

"Trainer for Kathlyn or not, you're still *my* trainer. I am not one of Kathlyn's students, so she can't say anything." Anissa's determination showed in her tone.

Liam regarded her seriously. "She can if I'm doing it on her property while on the job."

"Then we could train after your work is done for the day."

"It's still her property, and I would still have to have clearance from her."

"Then I will convince her to give you *clearance*." She had an edge to her voice when she uttered the last word. Oh, why hadn't Uncle Liam just stayed in Sylacauga? This job did not even make sense. They had to commute from Sylacauga to a small-town stable that paid less and was about half the size. Now, even her training was in jeopardy.

"Clearance for what?" Kathlyn walked down the aisle toward them.

"Where's Kyrsten?" Anissa frowned.

"My office listening to music. Clearance for what?"

Anissa glanced at her uncle. He only shook his head to indicate this was her deal, not his. She took a deep breath and faced Kathlyn. "Clearance for me to continue my training."

Kathlyn raised one eyebrow. "I believe all you need to do is put your name on the student roster. Once that's done, we'll start your training."

"No. I want to *continue* my training. Not start. My Uncle Liam is my instructor and has been for the last six years."

"Liam does not work as an instructor here yet, though the plan is for him to work toward that. Also, the other girls will not agree to switch instructors all the sudden."

Anissa shook her head. "I do not want to ride with the other girls. Even in Sylacauga, Uncle Liam trained Rawad and me solo."

"And why is that?"

"Because when I started, Rawad was a young colt with zero training."

Kathlyn thought a moment. "Why don't you give me a couple days to consider it? Until then, you can continue to practice in the arena. I will let you know very soon, okay? Now, please go check on Kyrsten? I have a few things to do before going back to the office, and I know she enjoys your company."

Anissa grimaced but obeyed.

Kathlyn waited until the girl was well out of earshot before turning to her newest worker. "Liam, do you know why she is so insistent to train alone with you? I thought she had become friends with the other girls."

Liam exited Hawk's stall, latching the half-door behind him. "Anissa used to be a very sweet, friendly girl. She was outgoing and knew no strangers. Alot changed when my brother, her father, died. She drew into herself, and no one could draw her back out. She became friends with Kyrsten right after the accident, and has seemed to really enjoy having a close friend. When she got Rawad, she actually began to return to her old self. But, she's become slightly hostile ever since I announced my job change. I asked if she wanted to talk about it, but she refused. I don't honestly know how to help her." Liam fell silent then.

Kathlyn nodded. "Thank you for telling me. I will speak to you again before I inform her of a decision."

"Thank you."

Kathlyn had decided to allow Anissa to train under her Uncle Liam at least until school began, at which time the situation would be re-discussed.

So today, Anissa was going to do a session with her uncle before heading over to Kyrsten's house. She was whistling a happy tune as she tacked up Rawad, glad to be on her regular training regime again.

"You are the spittin' image of your father like that."

Anissa startled. Where had he come from? She faced her uncle with raised eyebrows.

"Minus the long hair of course." He smirked. He stood against the wall outside Rawad's stall with his arms crossed. He continued, "I can't count how many times I heard him whistling something or other while he worked; never stopped to take a breath most days. Told me he loved his job so much he couldn't help but whistle about it."

There was a pang in her chest. Yes, her daddy had loved his job. He had always come home laughing and smiling. And he had whistled around the house alot too. Sometimes she could still hear him in her head, whistling while helping her mom. "Do you still miss him?" she whispered.

Liam closed his eyes, then opened them. "Of course. Every day," he said in a strained voice. "He was the best brother I could have. And not just my brother: my friend, confidant. The closest and most important person in the world to me."

Anissa felt a catch in her throat. She did not speak as she stood there, fighting to keep the tears at bay.

After a few moments of silence, Liam spoke softly, "I'll meet you in the ring in five, okay?"

Anissa managed to nod; Liam left her alone.

As she prepared to take Rawad to the arena, she was still thinking of her Father. While he had whistled more than anything, he had also sung a few songs. Anissa could remember some of the lyrics from the one he had sung to her as a child when she was scared or unsettled. She had only ever heard her dad sing the song.

My Lord, He calls me
He calls me by the thunder
The trumpet sounds within-a my soul
I ain't got long to stay here

Chapter 12: New Lessons

A wise man is strong; yea, a man of knowledge increaseth strength. ~Proverbs 24:05

Madison became curious. "Kathlyn, why did we have to get here early and find an empty row to sit on?" She had to look over her daughter's head to ask the question.

"That's why." Kathlyn pointed at a large group of people making their way towards the row Kathlyn had chosen.

"Hi, Kyrsten!" Hilary said when she reached earshot. "Hey, Kathlyn!"

"Hello, Hilary. This is Madison, Kyrsten's mother," Kathlyn responded, gesturing to the woman on Kyrsten's right.

DJ, Hilary, and their families found seats with the two girls and Katya closest to Kathlyn.

"These are our families." Pointing at each person as she spoke, DJ introduced, "My parents, Dora and Dave, my brother, David, my baby sister, Dorothy, and my grandparents, Marga and Daniel. Hilary's parents are Irene and Simon, her sister, Katya, and the other boy is Katya's friend, Alyosha Preobrazhensky."

"Nice to meet y'all." Madison murmured politely.

After service, Kathlyn touched Kyrsten's shoulder. "Hey, I'm taking Hilary and DJ to lunch; do you want to come?"

Kyrsten was hesitant. Anissa would not be there, and Kyrsten wasn't sure she knew Hilary and DJ all that well. "Is Mom okay with it?"

"Yes, I've already checked with her." Kathlyn saw Kyrsten's hesitation. "You don't have to come if you don't want to, but it would be a great chance for you to get to know the other girls better. You're not around them as much as Anissa is."

"Okay," Kyrsten finally agreed.

"Alright, let's go then." Kathlyn grinned.

They had barely been seated in the restaurant when Hilary saw someone she recognized.

"Mr. Dobrynin!!" Hilary got up and ran to meet the man being led to an empty table.

"Miss Hilary!" Grinning broadly, he hugged her. "How are you?"

"Good! Come sit with us!" Hilary begged.

"Are you sure the other members in your party are okay with that?" Lyle allowed her to lead him to the table.

"Kathlyn, can Mr. Dobrynin sit with us?" Hilary asked hopefully.

Kathlyn glanced uncertainly at Kyrsten. "What do y'all want, Kyrsten and DJ?"

"I'm cool with it," DJ readily responded.

"Kyrsten?" Kathlyn tapped the hand the girl had placed on the table.

"I don't care," Kyrsten's answer was barely audible.

"That's fine, Hilary." Kathlyn gestured for Lyle to take a seat.

"Mr. Dobrynin, this is DJ and Kathlyn; I told you about them when I showed you my Bible at school awhile back. The girl beside Kathlyn is Kyrsten. She moved to Shorter from Sylacauga."

Lyle chuckled. "Nice to meet y'all. How do you like it in Shorter, Miss Kyrsten?"

Kyrsten didn't respond.

Kathlyn wondered if she should have politely said it was a girls' outing. Now that Lyle had joined them, Kyrsten refused to speak.

After lunch, the four girls were getting up to leave when Mr. Dobrynin pulled Kathlyn aside. "Is the girl blind?" he asked.

"Yes; you figured that out fast." Kathlyn frowned slightly.

Lyle smiled reassuringly. "My niece is blind." He cleared his throat. "How recent is the blindness? And is it permanent?"

"Happened a few years ago. Yes, it is permanent."

"Have her parents set up a way to teach her to read and write?"

Kathlyn raised an eyebrow. "She's blind. She can't read. Her mother has decided to teach her at home orally."

"May I give you my number to give to her parents? Tell them that I can teach Kyrsten to read and write even though she is blind. My niece can do so well that she attends regular school and only her teachers and close friends realize she is blind."

Tuesday, July 05

"Hello, Anissa. Kyrsten is upstairs." Madison greeted their daily visitor.

"Thanks, Madison."

"Of course. I'll call y'all down for lunch in a few okay?"

"'Kay." Anissa ran up the stairs.

"Hi, Kyrsten." Anissa entered her friend's room without knocking since the door was open.

"Hi!" Kyrsten looked up. "After lunch, could you help me write another letter to my Dad?"

"Sure." Anissa got on the bed with her friend. "I have a question."

"What's that?"

"If I sing a few lines of a Christian song to you, would you recognize it?"

Kyrsten nodded. "If I've heard it before."

Without preamble, Anissa sang the lines from the song she'd remembered while at the stable several days ago. She'd forgotten to ask Kyrsten about it until now.

Kyrsten frowned thoughtfully when her friend finished. "I don't recognize it. I'm sorry. I guess I haven't heard it before."

Anissa was disappointed but only said, "That's okay."

"What is it from?"

"My... Daddy used to sing it to me."

"Then would your mom know it?"

"I sure hope so."

Holman Correctional Facility Atmore, Alabama:
Thursday, July 07

Kyrsten did not know whether to be excited or nervous. In a few minutes, she would get a chance to talk to her daddy. She had only gotten to come to the prison with her mom a few times. It had been over a year since she had last visited. Today was extra special because Kyrsten would be allowed to talk to her dad privately. No other people, not even her mom. Her mom would escort Kyrsten in, hug Justin, then wait in a hallway or something. Apparently, her daddy had a police friend who had helped arrange this. Kyrsten had not had the chance to talk freely with her dad since he was arrested. Now she would. She felt bad for her mother, though, but Madison had assured her it was okay since Madison had talked to Justin privately a couple times.

105

"We're here, Kyrsten. It'll be just a minute before your daddy arrives. Why don't you sit here?" Madison guided her daughter into the chair.

"How long will I be able to talk to him?"

"About twenty minutes, I think. The guard will come back in when the time is up. I'll come back in then, too."

Kyrsten did not respond. She could hear footsteps coming closer. There was a slight commotion as her daddy was led in and her mom got a chance to hug him before a guard had him sit down across from Kyrsten. Then Kyrsten was left alone with her father.

"Hey, Kyrsten." His voice washed over her like a sense of belonging.

"Hi, Daddy," she replied softly. "I really miss you."

"I have really missed you, too. I am so sorry I haven't been home for you." Emotion underscored Justin's words.

"It's not your fault."

"What have you been doing lately? Have you finished tutoring for the summer?"

"I finished early because my tutor moved to Tennessee."

"Oh, I hadn't heard."

"Anissa comes over almost every afternoon to hangout with me. Kathlyn comes over some too. She and Mommy have become good friends. I have a new album on my music player; it's by Highlands Worship. I really like the second song on the album."

"I'm glad you still love music," Justin commented quietly.

Kyrsten smiled. "The music is like an anchor."

"What do you mean?"

"Now that I can't see, everything seems disorienting. Even though my hearing has become fairly keen, alot is still just confusing. It makes me nervous to be in busy areas or around alot of people. I use the music as a reminder that Jesus loves me no matter what, and that He will protect me and give me peace."

"Sounds like being blind has made your Faith even stronger," he observed.

Kyrsten nodded. "I still miss being able to see. I wish I could see people's faces, especially yours. I miss being able to read or color."

"Your mother found one of your old colored pictures and gave it to me."

"Really?"

Justin nodded then caught himself. "Yes. It's of a grey horse in a barn."

"I don't like horses anymore."

"Why is that?"

Kyrsten only shrugged. "Daddy, my friend Anissa says she's a Christian, but she doesn't seem very sure or committed. If I ask why, she just brushes me off. What should I do? I wanted to ask you sooner, but she sees all my letters to you."

Justin thought a second. "Keep being an example to her. Maybe try to find a different approach. Pray for her, and I will also Pray."

"Okay."

They continued to talk, and all too soon the guard came back and their time was up. Kyrsten was allowed to hug her dad, and she clung tightly to him for several moments. She said a choked goodbye as the guard led him away.

"I love you, Kyrsten!" Justin told her.

"I love you, too, Daddy."

Anissa had stayed home in Sylacauga, since today was Carrie's off day. Anissa knew Kyrsten was visiting her dad that day, and Anissa was glad for her. But she also felt envious being unable to do something like that herself.

Thinking of Kyrsten, she suddenly remembered to ask her mom about the song her dad used to sing. On a mission, she immediately went to her mother's bedroom, remembering that Carrie had said she was straightening up the room.

Anissa stopped in the open doorway and knocked. "Mom?"

"Come in," Carrie said over her shoulder. She was on her knees trying to close the bottom drawer of her dresser. "Can you help me with this? I think it got off the track somehow."

"Sure." Anissa knelt beside her mom and helped get the drawer back on its track so that it would close correctly. With two people, the job was much easier and took only a minute.

"There." Carrie sat back on her heels. "Thank you, Anissa."

"You're welcome."

"Now, what did you need?" Carrie steadied herself by pressing the fingers of one hand to the floor.

"The other day I remembered part of a song that Daddy used to sing, but I don't know what it is. I was trying to see if you know."

"What do you remember of it?" Carrie stood up and beckoned for her daughter to follow her to the bed where they both sat side-by-side.

"I'm guessing it's just one verse of it." Anissa went over the lines she remembered.

"Yes, I remember that song. It's actually not a traditional song; it's a spiritual."

"A spiritual?"

"They are similar to hymns in length, but they aren't hymns. The spiritual was created by Africans enslaved to plantation owners. Simple verses that were easy to remember and easy to pass on."

"Do you know the name of that one?" Anissa asked hopefully.

"No, but I can find it for you." Carrie grabbed her laptop then settled back beside Anissa. She went to her search browser and typed in a couple lines of the spiritual. "It's called 'Steal Away To Jesus'," she announced. "Here, let's go downstairs to my office, and I'll print off the lyrics for you."

"Thanks, Mom."

"You're welcome, Sweetheart."

Tuesday, July 12

"Mr. Dobrynin, come in! What brings you here?" Irene opened the door wider to allow him entrance.

"Hello, Mrs. Seawright. How are you, today?" Lyle smiled.

"I'm good. Are you here to see the girls?"

"Actually, with your permission, I would love to take Hilary with me. I need her assistance teaching a class just down the road."

"A class?" Irene raised an eyebrow.

"I am going to teach a blind girl how to read and write. She lives not far from here, and I believe Hilary is friends with her."

"Oh, you must mean Kyrsten Levine." Irene walked to the bottom of the stairs. "Girls! Mr. Dobrynin is here."

The girls quickly came downstairs. "Hi, Mr. Dobrynin!" they greeted in unison.

"Hello, Miss Katya, Miss Hilary. If you don't mind, Miss Hilary, I could use your assistance today. I am going to start teaching Kyrsten Levine how to read and write even though she is blind."

"How can I help with that?" Hilary asked incredulously.

"You are friends with Miss Kyrsten, correct?"

Hilary nodded.

"I believe she will be more comfortable if she has a friend there. You could help ease tension, since she does not know me, but you do."

Hilary glanced at Irene questioningly.

"It's okay with me if you want to go." Irene nodded briefly.

"Okay, I'll go."

"Can I come too?" Katya requested.

"Of course, Miss Katya," Mr. Dobrynin quickly agreed.

At Kyrsten's house, Madison quickly let them in and led them upstairs. "Thank you so much for coming, Mr. Dobrynin. I hope Kyrsten will be receptive to this. I have not actually told her anything yet. She has said that she wants to learn how to do things even though she's blind, but it's all still so new."

"I understand," Lyle assured. "I brought the Seawright girls with me, because I hope that it will help her feel more comfortable."

Madison nodded. She knocked on a closed bedroom door.

"Come in," Kyrsten called softly.

Madison opened the door. "You have visitors, Kyrsten."

"Hi, Kyrsten!" Hilary's greeting was lively.

"Hilary! Is DJ here, too?" Kyrsten accepted Hilary's hug.

"Nope, but my sister is."

"Hey, Katya."

"Hello," Katya said as she briefly hugged Kyrsten.

Madison spoke up, "There is someone else here as well, Kyrsten. His name is Lyle Dobrynin. He has come to teach you a couple things."

"Hello, Miss Kyrsten."

"Hi."

"Mr. Dobrynin used to be both mine and Katya's schoolteacher when we were younger," Hilary inserted.

Lyle sat in the chair Madison brought him. "Miss Kyrsten, what do you want more than anything else in the world?"

Kyrsten did not respond.

"Miss Kyrsten, for this to work well, you will have to answer my questions honestly."

"You can trust him, Kyrsten," Katya assured as she sat down on the bed beside her newest friend.

Kyrsten took a deep breath. "My Dad," she whispered.

Mr. Dobrynin glanced at Madison in confusion.

"Her father is imprisoned for a crime he did not commit," Madison quietly explained.

"What if you could talk to him?" Lyle asked.

"He sent me a letter, but I can't talk to him." Kyrsten shrugged.

"What if you could write him a letter?"

"Anissa wrote one for me."

"What if you could write it yourself?" Lyle pressed.

Kyrsten frowned. "But I'm blind."

"My niece is blind. She goes to public school, she can read and write, and no one knows the difference."

"Really?" Kyrsten was afraid to hope.

"If you will work with me and be patient, if you will answer my questions when I ask them, I can help you learn to do the same as my niece."

Kyrsten hesitated.

"Go for it, Kyrsten," Hilary urged.

"We'll all help you; you can be sure of that." Katya touched Kyrsten's forearm.

"I'll do it." Kyrsten's tone carried more confidence than she felt.

"Then, let's get started." Lyle grinned broadly.

Chapter 13: Dressage Star

A wise man will hear, and will increase learning; and a man of understanding shall attain unto wise counsels: ~Proverbs 01:05

"Tell me you're getting closer to finding who framed me."

Jordan seemed to consider this. "Maybe."

"Maybe?" Justin sat back in his chair. "What does *maybe* mean? You're either close or not."

Jordan smiled sympathetically. "I said maybe. We'll get there when we get there. When the time comes, I'll let you know. Just be patient."

Justin grumbled under his breath.

"I heard that. Listen, I can't yet give you your freedom, but I asked the warden to sign you up for something."

Justin looked up. "What's that?"

"Work-release program. It'll get you out of here some days."

"What type of work?"

"You'll be part of a crew that helps clean up trash along the roads, especially along highways."

"Okay. When do I start?"

Jordan shrugged. "Soon. You'll know when the warden tells you to load up in the van with your crew." He grinned.

"Well, it's not like I have much else on my schedule. So long as it doesn't interfere with visits from you and my family."

"It shouldn't interfere."

"Thanks, Jordan. Really."

"You're welcome. And I'll keep looking into the charges against you."

Shorter, Alabama:
Thursday, July 14

Anissa turned Rawad in a tight circle, forcing herself to concentrate. She rode Rawad back to the side of the arena.

"Come on, 'Nissa, you can do this. Relax. Focus. Start over from the beginning." Uncle Liam leaned against the railing behind him.

Anissa nodded and took a deep breath. She urged Rawad into a collected trot, and they headed straight for the first marker, K. Once they reached the marker, she slowed him and did a large spiral between K and E. From the spiral, they moved into a free walk to C. Next, an extended trot to M, and a collected canter to F. They circled twice before heading to A at a working trot. At A, they halted, and the girl saluted her uncle.

A low whistle caught her attention, and she suddenly realized she had an audience. Hilary, DJ, and an older girl applauded her ride. Kathlyn stood behind the three girls with crossed arms and a wide smile, and a teenage boy, the one who'd whistled, saluted Anissa before walking into the stable.

"Very good, Anissa," Uncle Liam praised. "I believe that's the most focused I've seen you. You got slightly behind on your first circle, but recovered quickly. Also, you need to have more forward motion in that working trot."

Anissa let out a breath. "Yes, Sir."

"I have never seen someone ride like that," Hilary's eyes were wide.

"I think you could compete in high-level shows. You're the best dressage rider in this part of Alabama." DJ was completely serious.

Anissa could only grin. She rubbed Rawad's neck.

"Why didn't you sign up for dressage at the last show?" Kathlyn queried.

Anissa shrugged. "Nerves. I have trouble focusing."

"Keep working on it, and I would like you to start showing in dressage if that is agreeable to you?" Kathlyn raised an eyebrow.

"Alright." Her grin grew wider.

"Kathlyn, I want to ride like her." DJ smiled.

"It takes alot of hard work." Kathlyn uncrossed her arms.

"Alright, Anissa. Cool out Rawad; we're done for the day. Great job."

"Thanks, Uncle Liam."

After getting Rawad fully cooled off, Anissa dismounted and ran up her stirrups before exiting the arena. Her uncle had already gone inside, along with Kathlyn, but the three girls were waiting for Anissa.

"Anissa, remember my sister, Katya?" Hilary nodded to the older girl Anissa had not recognized. She now remembered the girl.

"Yeah."

"Kathlyn said you don't want to ride with us," Hilary said it without accusation.

DJ rolled her eyes. "She did not. Kathlyn's too nice to say it that way. She said, 'Anissa has chosen to train with her uncle as she did in Sylacauga'."

"Either way," Hilary insisted.

Anissa smiled in amusement. "I did not want to change instructors if I didn't have to."

"I can understand that," Hilary commented sensitively. "But we also want to spend time with you. By the time we get here each day, you're about to leave."

"True. I have to leave once I have Rawad fully taken care of."

"Exactly what I mean."

"Is there another way y'all could hang out? Besides riding I mean," Katya suggested.

"You could come over when we're all hanging out at either mine or Hilary's house," DJ invited.

"Maybe, but I do my best to spend all my extra time with Kyrsten."

DJ shrugged. "Bring her along. She's just as welcome to hangout as you are."

"That depends on Kyrsten." Anissa started towards the stable, leading Rawad.

The three girls followed her. "What is your horse's name?" Katya asked.

"Rawad."

"Where did you come up with that name?"

"It's Arabic for 'pioneer'. My Daddy's name is Rawad."

"That's really cool! Does your dad like to ride?"

"Her dad died," DJ quietly supplied.

Anissa answered the question anyway. "Yes, he worked at the stable in Sylacauga for years. He loved to ride and train horses. My Uncle Liam and I still have his horse. Zane's stall is there to the right of Rawad's." Anissa nodded at Zane's stall, and she led Rawad into his own so she could untack him.

"Is your uncle's horse the one on the left?" Hilary asked as they said hello to Zane.

"The left of Rawad? Yes, that's Hawk," Anissa responded as she removed Rawad's saddle.

"Girls?" Kathlyn and Liam joined them. "I have a proposition for y'all. Nobody speak until I am finished."

The girls all stopped and faced Kathlyn. Anissa came out of Rawad's stall.

"Seeing Anissa's ride today made me realize that Liam is a better dressage instructor than I'll ever be. Liam has agreed to teach dressage for any students who wish to reach higher levels than I teach. I can teach advanced jumping, but not advanced dressage. The three of y'all ride daily, although Wednesdays and Sundays y'all are left to yourselves to practice. I recommend that DJ and Hilary take at least two dressage lessons from Liam each week, two jumping, one cross-country and one show jumping, under me, and one Western under me. And Anissa, if you would be willing to at least work afternoons on Saturdays, since I understand Liam has never put you in a Western saddle."

"Saturdays, but that's it," Anissa conceded.

"But what about Anissa's jumping?" Hilary frowned.

"She will continue under Liam unless she decides she wants advanced jumping," Kathlyn's tone brooked no argument.

Saturday, July 16

Having little to do each day, Kyrsten had asked her mom if they could have Kathlyn and Anissa over at her house on Tuesday evening. Anissa had, in turn, asked if she could invite DJ and Hilary, remembering the girls' complaint about not getting to hangout. Now, on Saturday, the girls, including Kathlyn and Katya, were gathered in Kyrsten's bedroom talking.

"Kyrsten, Hilary says you are going to learn to read and write," Anissa commented.

Kyrsten nodded. "Mr. Lyle was at my house yesterday to start teaching me."

"Wait, I didn't know that," Kathlyn spoke up.

117

"Kaari and I went with him. Because he thought Kyrsi would be more comfortable if someone she knew was there," Hilary supplied. The group, Kathlyn, Anissa, DJ, Kyrsten, Hilary, and Katya, were all gathered at Hilary and Katya's house this time.

"I think he called my Mom, and she agreed to have him come." Kyrsten shrugged. "He says it'll take awhile, but he thinks I can do it."

"That's awesome, Kyrsten!" Kathlyn praised.

"We should build like a group," DJ suddenly suggested. "Like, we all hang out together all the time anyway. We could all work projects together, and be accountability partners for each other," she tried to explain. "Like the small groups at church."

"What kind of projects?" Anissa questioned.

DJ shrugged.

Hilary and Katya traded a glance. Hilary raised a questioning eyebrow, and Katya nodded in response. Taking it as a go ahead, Hilary spoke up. "Katya and I actually started something similar to what you're talking about several years ago. It was just the two of us, but we could expand it basically to include everyone here," she ventured.

"Do y'all have a name for what y'all built together?" Kathlyn asked.

The sisters shook their heads. "No, but we have secret names." Katya grinned mysteriously.

"Really?" This came from Kyrsten.

"Yes, we created them using our first and middle names," Hilary supplied.

"But, the catch is that they have to be real names. Like you can look them up, and they have a meaning," Katya added.

"What *are* y'all's secret names?" Kyrsten could not wait any longer to ask.

Katya laughed. "I'm Kaari, from Katya Ariadne, and Hilary is Hira, from Hilary Rajiyah."

"Y'all's middle names are cool," Anissa commented.

"How do y'all create the secret names?" Kathlyn wanted to know.

Katya replied, "I created them using the first two to three letters of both the first and middle names. And the secret name itself has to be four to five letters in length only. For example, Kaari is five letters: K-a-a-r-i, and Hira is four: H-i-r-a."

"Let's do it!" Anissa said suddenly.

The girls then got to work figuring out names. Anissa decided on Anela from Anissa Elaine, Kyrsten chose to go with Kyrsi from Kyrsten Ingryda, and Dinah Jane stuck with DJ, refusing to give herself another nickname.

"Is it okay that I used four letters from Kyrsten and only one from my middle name?" Kyrsten asked hesitantly.

Katya shrugged. "Sure."

"Kathlyn, what about you?" Anissa asked with a grin.

Kathlyn smiled. "I have thought about it, and I don't believe I can create a good name that meets all of the requirements. But, I have an idea, provided y'all will allow my name to have a sixth letter."

"What is the name?" Katya queried.

"Eirdis. It's my middle name."

"That's your middle name?!" Anissa raised an eyebrow.

"It's pretty!" Hilary declared.

"Works with me." Katya shrugged.

DJ nodded.

119

"Sounds good, then. That's what I will use." Kathlyn chuckled.

"I have an idea. Everyone name one thing you love," Anissa suggested.

"Easy. Horses, obviously," DJ said it as if they knew, which they did.

"Writing stories," Katya stated.

"I love to read, and I love to ride." This came from Hilary.

"I love music. My favorite song is 'Tremble', by Mosaic MSC," Kyrsten offered.

"The one we sang at church the other day?" Anissa perked up.

"Yes."

"Hmm. I love my horse, Rawad. So, horses again." Anissa grinned slightly. She looked to Kathlyn.

Kathlyn turned the tables on them. "I love you girls."

Chapter 14: Сторонник

Monday,
July 18, 2016

Iron sharpeneth iron; so a man sharpeneth the countenance of his friend. ~*Proverbs 27:17*

"Look, Anissa. Let's stop here to eat."

Anissa looked out the window at the restaurant her mother indicated. "Okay," she said as the vehicle began to pull into the parking lot.

Anissa, her mother, and Uncle Liam had driven down south to Mobile to see a Blue Angel show. Anissa had wanted to see the Blue Angels for years! The show had been awesome! It was insane watching all the cool moves they could do at such great speeds. There for a minute, it had gotten really loud as the FA-18 Hornets did a low flyover. Anissa had been really sad when the show ended.

They were now on the way home, and her mom had decided they should find a place to eat. They had left Mobile like an hour ago, so Anissa had no clue where they were now.

They entered the restaurant and were greeted by a hostess. "Would y'all like to sit inside or outside?"

"Outside, please," Carrie replied.

"Right this way."

The hostess seated them at a table, and then left after promising a waitress would be by shortly.

"Mom, where are we?"

"Why Anissa, don't you know what a restaurant is?" Uncle Liam cut in with a grin.

"We are in an area called Atmore; we're about an hour northeast from Mobile."

For some reason, the name of the city rang a bell in the back of Anissa's mind, but she couldn't figure out why.

"Hey, 'Nissa. While we're waiting on our food, do you want to cross the road with me to check out that store over there?" Uncle Liam pointed across the two-lane road.

"Sure."

The store proved to be not quite as interesting as they hoped, but it still passed time to look around.

They started crossing the road to head back, and Anissa noticed several men in orange cleaning up trash alongside the road. She could read the letters DOC on the back of one man's shirt. She turned to ask her uncle what the letters stood for and suddenly realized that she'd been paying more attention to the workers than to her surroundings. Her uncle was on the other side already, waving for her to hurry up. She lengthened her stride, noticing a rumbling noise to her left.

She had to stop in the middle of the road while four cars passed between her and her uncle. The rumble grew louder, and she looked to the left. Horror froze her when she saw the eighteen-wheeler bearing down on her.

"Anissa!!"

She was barely aware of her mom's scream as a pair of strong arms grabbed her and carried her to safety on the restaurant's side of the road.

The eighteen-wheeler passed as she was being transported over the other lane. Two seconds more, and she would have been dead.

"Anissa!" her uncle wrapped his arms around her as she sank to her knees on the other side of the road.

"I'm sorry. I couldn't move!" Anissa felt tears fill her eyes. She was shaking like a leaf.

"I thought you were behind me heading back to the restaurant; then Carrie screamed, and..." Uncle Liam swallowed, "I was too far away. I shoulda made sure you were behind me. I shoulda—"

"Anissa!" Carrie had run over from the restaurant and now knelt down beside her daughter. She hugged Anissa close. "I almost lost you! I was so scared!!" She was sobbing, and had to forcibly calm herself down so she could breathe.

"He saved me, Mom."

Carrie looked up at the man still standing near Anissa, quietly observing the family reunion. "Thank you, for rescuing my daughter."

Anissa got up and turned to face him. She realized he was one of the roadside workers she had seen. "Thank you."

He smiled. "You're welcome. I'm just glad you're okay. I need to get back to work." He turned to go.

"Wait! What's your name?"

The man faced her. "Justin. And you?"

Now, Anissa knew why Atmore had sounded familiar. It was on the address of all the letters she had helped Kyrsten with. This man wore orange because he was a prisoner. "Are you Kyrsten's dad?" she asked excitedly.

Justin's eyes widened. "You know Kyrsten?"

"Yes. I'm Anissa. I help her write letters to you. We've been best friends for years."

"I can't believe this! I had no idea it was you!"

Anissa grinned. "I will have to tell Kyrsten."

"Yes, and give her a hug for me."

"I definitely will!"

"Levine, let's go!" a prisoner guard near the road shouted.

"Good to finally meet you, Anissa." Justin waved before jogging over to the prisoner guard.

Anissa hugged her mom, still amazed that her rescuer turned out to be Kyrsten's dad. Wait till Kyrsten heard about this! What a day!

123

Kyrsten still could not believe that Anissa had met her dad yesterday. Anissa had told her and Madison about it earlier that afternoon. Right before that, she had announced they were invited over to Hilary's house for a "group meeting/hangout". The girls had just now gathered in Katya's bedroom upstairs.

"Hey, Kyrsten—" Kathlyn began.

"Kyrsi," Katya corrected. "There was no point in creating names if we're not going to use them."

Hilary giggled. Katya's tone was so stern!

"Sor-ry," Kathlyn drew out the word as she apologized sarcastically.

Katya grinned.

"It's going to be interesting having to know when to use the nicknames and when to used our regular names." Anissa played with her own hair.

"And y'all wonder why I didn't want a name besides DJ." DJ shook her head and rolled her eyes.

"You get used to it, eventually," Hilary responded to Anissa.

A knock sounded just before the bedroom door opened.

"Am I interrupting?"

Katya scrambled to her feet. "Alyosha! I didn't think you were coming over this afternoon!" She hugged him.

Alyosha put his hands in his pockets and shrugged. "I got off work early, today. What are y'all doing?"

"We're having a meeting. Remember I told you we created a girls' group?"

Alyosha nodded.

"You told him?" Anissa frowned. "I thought it was more of a secret."

"He's my best friend!" Katya got defensive.

Alyosha put his right forearm on Katya's shoulder, and leaned slightly toward her. He spoke in a tone as if confiding a secret, "Katya, how dare you tell me about y'all's oh-so-secret girls' group?"

Katya punched him in the ribs.

"Ow!" Alyosha pulled away.

"You're welcome."

"What is *that* supposed to mean?"

Katya only grinned and returned to her seat.

Alyosha shook his head in mock exasperation, making some of the girls chuckle. Alyosha chuckled as well. "Well, I'll leave y'all to y'all's 'secret meeting'." He put air quotes around the last two words.

"Close the door on your way out," Anissa instructed.

Without responding verbally, Alyosha saluted smartly and did as asked.

As soon as he left, the girls immediately started talking.

"We should find some Bible Verses about friends," Kathlyn suggested.

"'A friend loveth at all times, but a brother is born for adversity'," Kyrsten quoted.

"I know that one! Isn't it from Proverbs?" DJ asked.

Kyrsten nodded. "Proverbs 17:17."

"Very good, Kyrsi!" Kathlyn smiled. "Anyone else?"

"Isn't there another Verse in Proverbs that's about friends?" Hilary queried.

"Yes, but I don't know where it is. I can't quote it either," Kyrsten replied.

"Are y'all talking about Proverbs 18: 24?" Katya questioned.

"I believe Kaari is right," Kathlyn inserted.

"'A man that hath friends must shew himself friendly: and there is a friend that sticketh closer than a brother'," Katya quoted slowly.

"That's it," Hilary agreed.

"There's another I would like y'all to know." This came from Kathlyn again. "'Greater love hath no man than this, that a man lay down his life for his friends.' ~John 15:13."

"I like that one," Anissa commented.

"This is not a Bible Verse, but I thought of something," Katya began. "In Russian, the word for friend is сторонник *(storonnik).* It doesn't just mean friend, though; it means defender, believer, cohort, supporter, advocate, upholder, sympathizer, etc."

"That's really cool," Anissa said thoughtfully.

"Are there other languages that the word for friend has a deeper meaning?" Hilary wondered aloud.

"Why don't I look?" Kathlyn picked up her phone and ran a quick search. "In Arabic, the word for friend is حبيب *(habib)*, and it directly translates to beloved." She kept looking. "This is interesting. I don't know if this word actually is used for friend, but it still popped up. It's Norwegian and Danish. The word is naerhet, and it means closeness and intimacy. They said that it signifies an emotional intimacy versus physical."

"Hmm. Interesting for sure." Hilary thought about what Kathlyn had read.

The girls continued talking about friendship and what it really meant. It was awhile before Katya dared to ask, "I have a slightly off-subject question. Who decided our group has to be all girls??"

Everyone was silent.

"I guess we all just assumed that," Anissa finally said.

"Then is the group actually girls only?" Katya ventured.

Kathlyn surveyed the group. "How about we take a vote? Anyone who wants this to be girls only, raise y'all's hands."

Anissa immediately raised her hand. She was followed by both Kyrsten and DJ.

"Alright, who wants it to be girls and boys?"

Katya raised her hand, and Hilary and Kathlyn followed suit.

Kathlyn chuckled. "I believe we're tied. How about each person explain the reason behind their decision, and we'll all decide from there. My choice was boys and girls because I don't want y'all to turn away from good friendships just because it's a boy, and you're thinking that he can't join the group so why get close?"

"We can have friends outside the group. The group is just for special friends," Anissa pointed out argumentatively.

"Who says a boy couldn't be a special friend?" Katya fired back.

"Kaari is right," Kathlyn's tone was gentle, yet firm.

"Thank you, Eirdis." Katya took a breath. "My choice is the same as Eirdis'. I happen to have a very special friend who means alot to me. I want him to join the group."

Kathlyn nodded. She'd already known that was Katya's reason. "Hira, what about you? You chose same as Kaari and I."

Hilary shrugged. "I mainly chose that for Kaari's sake. But, while I enjoy having just girls, it's true that boys can be good friends, too. Alyosha is proof of that."

Katya leaned over to hug her sister.

"Now for the girls-only side. Anela?" Kathlyn raised an eyebrow at her newest riding student.

"I have never gotten along well with boys," Anissa replied vaguely. In all reality, she hated having to listen to boys talk about big dreams. Their dreams and male bravado reminded her too much of all her dad had never gotten a chance to do.

Kathlyn gave Anissa a look. She knew there was more than what the girl had shared. "Kyrsi?"

Kyrsten hesitated. "I know they shouldn't, but guys intimidate me, so I tend to avoid them. It's gotten worse since I became blind."

Hilary liked this new friend. Her honesty was refreshing.

DJ spoke up. "Y'all, I have a younger brother. Trust me; we do not want to allow boys into this group."

"DJ." Hilary's tone carried a hint of reprimand.

Kathlyn thought a moment. "Girls, are y'all willing to trust me? I believe we should allow boys the option to join. Anela's and DJ's reasons don't carry enough weight to hold any ground. Kyrsi, if you know the person, you probably would not be quite so intimidated; plus, we'll all always be close to you."

Kyrsten nodded slowly.

"I am going to create a restriction, though," Kathlyn continued. "Before any person, girl or boy, is accepted as a member, they can come to one meeting to try it out. It will give them a chance to see if they really want to join, and give us a chance to figure out how comfortable we would be if they were around all the time."

Chapter 15: Breakthrough

Thursday,
July 21, 2016

I know thy works: behold, I have set before thee an open door, and no man can shut it: for thou hast a little strength, and hast kept My word, and hast not denied My Name. ~Revelation 03:08

With a sigh, Jordan sat back in his chair and rubbed the grit from his eyes. Today, he had only had to work a half day, and he had spent his entire afternoon off looking more into Justin's case.

While he could find some flaws in documentation, they were all very minor. He had yet to prove that Justin had not done it beyond a shadow of a doubt. If someone had framed Justin, they had done it remotely and covered their tracks well.

Exasperated, Jordan got up and stalked to his kitchen to get a drink. This case had him baffled; he had spent months on it with no definite leads. He hated seeing Justin's hope and following disappointment each time Jordan visited the prison.

He closed his refrigerator door after grabbing a Dr. Pepper. The framed picture that was top-center of the door caught his eye. A picture of him throwing his baby girl up in the air. The picture which showed them so carefree had ironically been taken the day before his wife left, taking their daughter with her. Talk about baffling.

It was because of Jordan's daughter that he had even decided to help Justin. Now, he was doing it for the little girl who missed her daddy, for the wife who believed in her husband.

Walking back to the living room, Jordan tried to think of a new angle. He sat down in front of his computer. There had to be something he was missing. He had even tried following the trail as if he were the perpetrator, but he had not found anything. He was not much of a computer guy; that probably had something to do with it.

He glared at the computer in front of him. He should probably just call it a night. He was starting to have trouble focusing, and he had to get up early for work in the morning.

Why would someone frame a DMV worker for white collar crimes? Justin was sure no one held a grudge against him. So, had it been random chance that Justin was the one framed? What if there was a simple solution to all of this?

Suddenly, Jordan sat straighter. He navigated to a new window on his computer. Quickly pulling up the file he was looking for, he scanned through the list of numbers displayed there. Sure enough, there was a discrepancy. He grabbed his cellphone and dialed the detective in charge of Justin's case.

"Hey, I found something you should be aware of."

"This the same case as last time you called?" The detective's tone was tired, gruff.

"Yes, Sir, it is. There's a discrepancy in some of the numbers. I'm emailing you the specific file I'm referring to."

Jordan fervently hoped this was the break Justin needed.

Shorter, Alabama:
Friday, July 22

"Very good, Miss Kyrsten!" Mr. Dobrynin praised.

"Did I get it?"

"Yes, you most certainly did! That's one to show your mother."

"Really? Awesome!"

Kyrsten had been working hard on learning to form her letters cleanly. Mr. Dobrynin had her write the alphabet over and over in both print and cursive. Although, cursive would be easier since she had to pick up her hand less, he wanted her to write well both ways.

Now, Kyrsten had finally written out the full alphabet both ways legibly and with even spacing.

"Do it again, Miss Kyrsten. Now, the goal will be consistency. You have already improved enough that you can start writing sentences by yourself next lesson."

Kyrsten nodded and got back to work. "Mr. Dobrynin?"

"Yes, Miss Kyrsten."

"Before you leave today, could you help me write a letter to my Dad?"

"You mean you write it, with me showing you where each word starts as we've done in lessons?"

"Yes."

"Certainly, we will do that. Your father will be pleased, I'm sure."

"I have the second alphabet done."

Mr. Dobrynin took the paper. "I'm impressed. Amazing work. Let's work on reading for awhile; after which we will write your letter."

"Okay."

Instead of learning only braille like most people who had lost their sight, Kyrsten was also learning how to read raised print. That way she could attend regular public school. There was a company Lyle had found that produced all the regular school textbooks, as well as some novels, in raised print, which was absolutely perfect for Kyrsten and for Lyle's niece. Kyrsten already had a raised print Bible.

After reading practice, which was much harder than writing, they composed a lengthy letter to Kyrsten's dad. At the end, she added a post script.

P.S. With some help from my tutor, I have written this letter myself. Next time, I'll write without help!

"Miss Kyrsten, I have a gift for you."

"What is it?" Her eyes showed interest.

"I found coloring books with raised lines since you told me how much you miss being able to color."

"Oh, wow! Really?"

"Yes, Ma'am." He handed her two tactile coloring books. "Enjoy them. And show your mother the papers with your handwritten alphabets."

"I will. 'Bye, Mr. Dobrynin."

"Goodbye. See you soon."

Saturday, July 23

Anissa grunted as she hefted the Western saddle over Rawad's back. The saddle landed sideways, so she pulled on it to shift it. Instead of shifting over the saddle pad, the weight made the saddle pad move *with* the saddle, so now the pad was crooked and the saddle was straight. She groaned in frustration.

"Having some difficulties, I see." Kathlyn walked into Rawad's stall.

"This blasted Western saddle!" Anissa cried.

"May I?" Kathlyn reached for the saddle.

"Knock yourself out." Anissa gestured in a go-ahead.

Kathlyn removed the saddle from Rawad's back. "Two things you can do. One is to have a helper hold the pad still until you get the hang of positioning the saddle over it. The other, which needs no helper, is to place the saddle over the pad and throw the whole pair up at once.

Like this," Kathlyn pulled the saddle pad off Rawad and deposited it on the stall door. Next, she grabbed the saddle and set it over the pad. She then grabbed the assemblage by the two ends and tossed it up onto the horse's back. "There you go!" Kathlyn grinned cheerily. "See you in ten." She left for the arena.

Almost ten minutes later, Anissa entered the arena for her second ever Western riding lesson. Kathlyn stood in the middle of the ring, and the other girls, Hilary and DJ, were mounted up by the railing.

Anissa mounted Rawad. "Sorry I'm late."

"You are not late; the girls are early," Kathlyn reassured. "Now, let's begin."

Anissa did her best to focus as Kathlyn gave them various instructions, but she was struggling. English riding was so much easier!

Everything seemed different for Western riding. Different saddle and gear. Different commands. Different gaits even. Anissa did not understand why she had to learn all of this. It wasn't like she had any dreams of being a cowgirl.

"Girls, move into an easy jog," Kathlyn instructed.

A jog? Was that like a trot? Anissa watched to see what the other two did. Which, of course, got her left behind.

"Jog, Anissa!" Kathlyn repeated.

"I. Don't. Get. This!" Anissa growled. She pulled Rawad to a halt and dismounted. "I'm done." She opened the gate.

"Anissa! Please mount now." The order was unmistakable.

"No!" Anissa tugged Rawad into a fast walk as she hurried to the barn.

"Let's call it a day, Girls." Kathlyn sighed. "I'll do a slightly longer lesson next week to make up for this. Right now, I need to go talk to Anissa."

"We understand, Kathlyn." DJ dismounted.

"I think something is wrong besides the new riding regime." Hilary dismounted as well, concern filling her face.

Kathlyn found Anissa in Rawad's stall. The stall door was closed, Rawad was still tacked up, and Anissa was in the back corner with her head on her knees.

Kathlyn entered the stall. "You want to talk about it?" She knelt in front of Anissa.

"No. Go away." Anissa's tone was curt.

"I can't do that." Kathlyn allowed silence to prolong between them for a few moments. "You know I can relate to some of what you're going through."

"No, you don't."

"I lost my Mom."

Now, she had Anissa's attention. "Really?" The question was a whisper.

"Really."

"Did she die?"

"No, she's very much alive. She left when I was about ten. Never looked back. She broke all contact with our family. It was like we were of no consequence."

"Maybe she regrets it, now."

"I wish that were true."

Anissa looked up at her. "It doesn't really seem to bother you."

"It does. But it's been a long time, and I've learned how to deal with it. See, I struggled for a long time with the abandonment. I felt alone and unworthy. My Dad tried to fill that empty space left by my Mom, but it's not the same."

"I know what you mean." Her statement was barely audible.

"You've heard about Kyrsten's dad, Justin."

Anissa nodded.

Kathlyn continued, "Well, Justin's mom ended up mentoring me through my teenage years. It changed alot for me. The things she taught me shaped who I am today. Anyway, said all that to say: it will get better. And I want you to know you're not alone. You have me, your mom, DJ, Hilary, Kyrsten, Katya. And if you ever need anything, we're all here for you."

"Did you ever start to forget details about your mom?"

"No. The pain became less difficult, but it was still there. And no, I never forgot anything about her."

"I'm so scared that the longer he's gone, I'll start forgetting things. It'd be like losing him all over again." Tears filled Anissa's eyes.

Kathlyn leaned forward and wrapped her arms around the girl. "I can't promise you that you'll never forget a thing, but what I can promise you is this: No matter what, your daddy loves you, and one day you *will* see him again. And you can always ask God to keep your memories fresh. He cares about every detail of our lives, especially our treasured memories. Your memory is worth more than all the riches in the world."

They sat there a moment until Anissa pulled away to dry her face. "Thanks, Kathlyn."

Kathlyn smiled. "Would you like help with untacking?"

"Sure." They both got up. "Why do I have to learn Western riding?"

"It helps you become a better all-around rider; plus, it's great for trail riding. There's alot of U.S. history tied to it as well."

Anissa wrinkled her nose. "History puts me in mind of school. School and riding do not mix."

Kathlyn laughed. "Depends on the person. Some people like history."

"Ew. No way. You do realize it's July, right?"

Kathlyn laughed harder.

"*You* don't like history, do you?"

"The history of riding. And horses."

Anissa couldn't help grinning at that.

"Hey, you'll be at the meeting at my house on Monday, right?"

"Yeah. We've never met at your house before."

"I voted for my house. Alyosha is coming for the first time, and I decided my house would be more neutral ground."

"That makes sense."

Monday, July 25

"Is Katya coming, Hilary?" Kyrsten asked.

DJ looked at her in surprise. "You could tell that Katya's not here?"

"She would have spoken by now if she were."

"But she's the quietest one besides you most of the time."

Kyrsten only shrugged.

"To answer your question, Kyrsten, she'll be here soon. She was waiting for Alyosha to get off work, and I went ahead and came with DJ."

"Hello!" Katya called from the entryway.

"In the living room!" Kathlyn replied loudly.

Katya entered the living room with Alyosha close behind her. "Sorry, we're late."

"Y'all are fine." Kathlyn assured.

"Welcome to the group, Alyosha," Hilary smiled.

"Thanks." He took a seat. "Hey, I hope it's okay: I invited a friend to join us today as well. You know, since y'all already were having a different style meeting today to decide if I could join."

"You invited another person?" Anissa frowned.

"Who?" Kyrsten asked.

"You'll see," Alyosha shrugged noncommittally.

Everyone looked at Katya questioningly. "I have no idea," Katya raised her hands in a I'm-backing-off gesture.

"Me neither," Hilary added.

Alyosha grinned.

"Is it a friend from work?"

"No."

A knock sounded on Kathlyn's front door.

"I shall get it. Please remain here." Kathlyn left the room. She returned with Alyosha's *friend* beside her.

DJ's mouth fell open. "David?! What are you doing here?"

David shrugged. "Alyosha invited me." He looked around uncertainly.

Kyrsten leaned closer to Anissa and whispered, "Do we know him?"

"DJ's brother," Anissa responded in a low tone.

"Sit down, Bro." Alyosha gestured to the seat on his left. Katya sat to his right.

David sat and glanced at his sister, trying to gauge her reaction to his presence. He decided it would be best to remain as quiet as he could. Unobtrusive.

"Okay." Kathlyn reclaimed her seat. "Let's see. Why don't y'all boys answer any questions the girls have; then y'all can ask us questions. That work?"

Several of them nodded.

Hilary raised her hand. "Are we asking them both together, or one at a time? And should we raise our hand each time we have a question?"

Kathlyn laughed. "Whatever suits you."

Katya nudged Alyosha. "Name one thing you love."

Alyosha raised an eyebrow. "Need you ask?"

"For the benefit of the group," Katya explained.

"Okay. Talking to random people I don't know."

"*What??*" Anissa tried not to laugh.

"Seriously. I like to walk up to people, introduce myself, and start a conversation. It's fun learning about the lives of the people you come in contact with daily. And sometimes, God will direct me to certain people to be a friend to them and/or help them out in some way."

"That's how we became friends, by the way," Katya interjected. "He was in line behind me in airport security."

"That's interesting," Kathlyn nodded. "What about you, David?"

David shifted in his seat. "I like to play basketball with friends."

"Do you play at school on the team?" Kyrsten braved the question.

David nodded in answer.

"If y'all boys would answer aloud each time, that would be appreciated," Kathlyn instructed politely.

"Okayyy. Yes, I play at school." David seemed confused.

"It's because I'm blind," Kyrsten's voice was barely audible.

"No one would know unless you told them," Alyosha said honestly.

"Why do both of y'all want to join the group?" DJ asked suddenly.

Alyosha answered first, "I would like the chance to spend more time with Katya, to spend time with all of y'all, and get to know y'all better. I believe no one can have too many friends and that having a circle of accountability partners is wise."

Anissa raised her eyebrows. Impressive. She realized then that they should not have judged these boys without knowing them.

Alyosha gestured for David to take his turn at answering.

"I honestly just came as Alyosha's friend. I would like to hangout with y'all more." He glanced at his sister. "But I do not intend to impose. I realize I'm not at all like y'all. Y'all don't have to accept me into y'all's inner circle."

DJ felt a twinge of guilt knowing that David's hesitancy and words were her fault.

Kathlyn felt sad. She had known DJ and David were dealing with some tension, but had not known the extent of it.

Sensing tension and wanting to end it, Hilary spoke up. "Do y'all boys have any questions for us?"

David shook his head. "No."

"Alyosha?"

Chapter 16: Turning Tides

Monday,
July 25, 2016

Have not I commanded thee? Be strong and of a good courage; be not afraid, neither be thou dismayed: for the LORD thy God is with thee whithersoever thou goest. ~Joshua 01:09

After the boys had left, it was time to decide whether they could join the group permanently or not. The girls put it to a vote.

Katya went first. "I vote yes. Both boys should join. They both are fun to hangout with, and both have their own areas of wisdom. They would bring alot to the group, I think."

"I vote no. The group should stay all girls." DJ crossed her arms.

"Alyosha makes me think of what my Dad would have been like at that age. I want him to join us. And if he's joining, David might as well too." Anissa shrugged.

Kyrsten was slightly hesitant. "I vote no. We still don't know them. David stayed quiet mostly, and Alyosha…"

"What Kyrsi?" Katya was already growing defensive.

"He's scary."

"Like intimidating?" Anissa clarified.

Kyrsten nodded.

"Eirdis?" Katya asked eagerly.

"I vote yes for both boys. I believe they could be great friends for all of us."

Katya nudged her sister. "Hira? You're the last to vote."

"Alyosha can join." Hilary confirmed.

"That's two votes against Alyosha and four votes for him," Anissa tallied aloud.

"What about David, Hira?" Kathlyn reminded.

Hilary was torn. DJ obviously did not want her brother to join, so out of loyalty to her, Hilary would say no. But Hilary felt bad for David, and she really wanted DJ's and David's relationship to mend. "I'd rather not vote on him," she said quietly.

"I think that's okay. David would have two against him and three for him without Hira's vote." Anissa glanced at Kathlyn for confirmation.

Kathlyn only nodded.

"So, both boys join!" Katya clapped once. "I'll text Alyosha right away. I don't have David's number, though."

"I have it," Hilary volunteered.

A few minutes later, everyone was getting ready to leave.

Kathlyn requested, "Hira, stay behind please."
"Okay."

After the others had left on their bikes and Kyrsten's mother had picked her up, Kathlyn sat beside Hilary. "Why didn't you want to vote on David?"

Hilary explained how she'd been conflicted.

"I thought it was something like that. Do you like or dislike David personally?"

Hilary shrugged. "I don't dislike him. I don't know him all that well either."

Kathlyn understood that. "It's always hard being caught in the middle of friends. Having loyalty to both sides makes decisions difficult. That's when you have to learn to make a decision based on the wisdom God has given you. The best leaders are those who can make a decision for the good of all, even when someone close to them doesn't like it."

"That's not easy."

"No, it's not. But with God, all things are possible."

Hilary changed the subject. "Hey, before I go, I want to present you with a DJ-style idea."

"So, is it your idea or DJ's?" Kathlyn asked teasingly.

"It's mine. It's just something similar to ideas DJ often comes up with," Hilary explained.

"Should I be worried?" Kathlyn was not a bit serious.

Hilary laughed. "No! It's a good idea, I promise."

Kathlyn chuckled. "Okay, so what is this new idea of yours?"

"We should all get together for dinner."

"When?"

"When everyone is all free at the same time."

"Who is everyone or all?"

Hilary grinned mischievously. "All our group and their families."

Kathlyn raised an eyebrow. "Do you know how many people that will be?"

Hilary giggled at Kathlyn's mock disbelief. "It will work! At least I think."

"Are you sure DJ is not in on this plan?" Kathlyn tilted her head consideringly.

"Promise!"

"How do you propose we have dinner with that many people? That's a tall order for a restaurant."

"I figured we'd use one of the families' houses, and everyone could contribute." Hilary presented this bit of her plan very businesslike.

Kathlyn nodded slowly. "Maybe. Let me think on it. Have you mentioned it to your parents or the other girls, yet?"

Hilary shook her head vigorously. "No. I figured you should be the first to know. Plus, since you're an adult, you should be the one to present the plan to all our parents."

"Do you want me to explain to them who first came up with this new scheme?"

"It's not a scheme; it's a plan for everyone to get to know each other better. And no, I don't need any credit for it."

"Oh, I see how it is! Use me to be sure it doesn't backfire, right?"

"Yes and no," Hilary tried to stifle another laugh.

Kathlyn shook her head in feigned exasperation. "We shall see," she promised vaguely.

Tuesday, July 26

"DJ, have you had lunch, yet?"

"Yes, Ma'am. I'm about to head to the stable."

"You be careful, you hear?" Marga grabbed her car keys.

"I will. You going somewhere?" DJ raised an eyebrow.

"David asked me to pick him up after basketball." Margaret and Daniel James were taking care of their grandkids while Dora and Dave went to a meeting.

DJ rolled her eyes.

Marga did not miss that. "What's happened with y'all? Y'all were very close up until the last month or so."

"Nothing," DJ avoided the question. "I have to go."

Sighing, Marga went upstairs to tell Daniel and Dorothy goodbye.

At the elementary school in Tuskegee, Marga walked to the basketball court. On the court, David and his friends were in the middle of some type of competition.

One of the boys dribbled the ball before tossing it to the basket. However, the ball did not make it into the basket as it was blocked by another boy.

143

"Come on! Score for us!" The boy who'd blocked the ball cheered.

"You know my grandmother taught me about crows when I was five. That's my whole life in half ago," David commented.

"What?!"

"He who crows first laughs last."

Marga chuckled.

"Your turn," David's friend threw the ball to a kid on the "opposing team". The kid tossed the ball to the basket successfully bypassing those trying to stop him. A boy on David's team jumped to stop the ball from entering the basket, but he was too late.

"That was slow!" David called. "Did you have Granny Smith apples for breakfast or something?"

"Or something," the boy replied.

"Your turn, David."

With a grin, David took the ball. He dribbled it in front of him as he darted around his friend before taking the shot. The ball made it in. "That's what I'm talking about!"

Marga smiled, delighted to see her grandson enjoying himself.

David spun around and caught sight of her. He waved before turning back to his friends. "I must leave y'all to it, since my grandmother is here. To keep a lady waiting is a serious offense, or so I've heard." He said his goodbyes, grabbed his stuff, and joined Marga on the sidelines. "Hi, Grandmother! Thanks for coming to get me."

"Of course." They walked to her car.

Once she'd pulled out of the parking lot, Marga asked, "David, what's going on between you and your sister?"

David sighed. "I don't know for sure."

"Any ideas?"

"No, Ma'am. I really wish I knew. I miss having her as a friend."

"I'll be praying, okay?"

"Thanks."

Wednesday, July 27

"David?"

David spun around almost dropping the bowl he held. DJ stood behind him. "You startled me."

DJ gave a half smile. "Sorry."

David set his bowl back on the counter. "What do you need?"

"I need to talk to you."

"Okay?" David walked past her to sit at the table.

"I haven't treated you very well, lately." She joined him at the table. I don't know what's gotten into me lately. After Dorothy was born, I guess I just felt like I wasn't important anymore. Mom and Dad are always busy or taking care of her. And on top of that, two girls in the group are obviously going through stuff but refuse to talk about it. I guess I just started taking it out on you; I'm so sorry, David."

"I forgive you. You know Dorothy hasn't replaced you, right?"

DJ nodded. "I know. Kathlyn and I talked about it yesterday."

"You should also talk to Mom and Dad."

"That's a great idea." The voice scared both kids.

Dave appeared in the kitchen doorway. "Sorry, but I heard the whole thing."

"Come in, Dad," David invited.

Dave sat down with them. "I'm glad y'all two are working things out."

145

"Of course, Dad. The whole point of this is just to fulfill your absolute delight." David tried to deepen his voice, so it ended up cracking instead.

Trying not to laugh, DJ snorted.

"That doesn't even make sense," Dave shook his head.

DJ and David laughed.

Thursday, July 28

Anissa knocked on Kathlyn's office door.

Kathlyn looked up. "Come on in."

Anissa did as bid and stood before the desk.

"What brings you here?" Kathlyn raised an eyebrow.

"Can people ride even if missing one of their senses?"

Kathlyn leaned back in her chair. "Lost one of their senses? You wouldn't happen to mean lost eyesight, would you?" She grinned.

"That's not fair! You always figure out hidden meanings too fast!"

Kathlyn laughed outright. "Anissa, have you met DJ? Or Hilary even? I have to think fast with those two."

"True, I guess," Anissa conceded.

"So, you want to know if there's a way that Kyrsten could ride despite being unable to see?"

"Yes, Ma'am."

"Yes, it's entirely possible. There are alot of great riders that are blind. Kyrsten's inability to see is not a problem."

"Then, I want to try to help her overcome her fear of horses. I think it would give her a huge confidence boost."

"I'm sure you're right. I am absolutely willing to help you, but in no way will we force Kyrsten's hand. She agrees to it of her own free will, or you can count me out. Forcing her will avail no improvement."

Anissa nodded. "I understand. We'll just have to convince her. Somehow. I could put her on Rawad if she agrees. He is very calm and responds to lighter signals."

"That's a good idea. Either Rawad or my training horse, Indie."

"Thanks, Kathlyn."

"You are welcome. Hey, how did the lesson go today?"

"Good. Uncle Liam keeps using me to demonstrate different maneuvers to DJ and Hilary. It's fun."

"Good. That will give you extra practice. And it will help you when you're showing."

"I guess I hadn't thought of that." Anissa tilted her head to the side.

"How have you been since our talk Saturday?"

Anissa hesitated. "Better."

Kathlyn could tell the girl was holding back. She pointed at the chair in front of her desk. "Sit."

Anissa obeyed.

"Now, what is it?"

"Nothing. Seriously." Anissa shook her head quickly.

"I don't believe that for a second."

She glanced down and remained quiet.

"I'm here if you need to talk."

"I know."

"Is there anything I can be praying for?"

Anissa just shrugged.

"Look, you can answer me now while we're alone, or I can bring this up in front of Kyrsten. You know she won't leave it be."

"She already doesn't leave it be. But y'all don't have to know everything."

Kathlyn saw a bit of the old rebellion in Anissa's eyes when the girl raised her head. "I'm not going to make you talk, but I will be here when you decide you're ready."

Anissa stood. "I need to go. I'll see you later."

Kathlyn said a silent prayer as she watched the girl walk out the door.

Her phone rang, surprising her. "Hello?"

The voice was automated. "Will you accept collect call from inmate—?"

"—Justin Levine." It was his voice.

"Yes." Kathlyn followed the instructions and was connected to her cousin. "Justin?"

"Hey, Kathlyn. How are you?"

"I'm good. Staying busy with the girls and the stable." She got up and closed her office door. "How are *you*?"

"Bored." He chuckled. "By 'the girls', do you mean student riders?"

"Yes. More specifically Kyrsten, Anissa, DJ, and Hilary. DJ and Hilary were students of mine way before Anissa started. Anissa is a friend of Kyrsten's."

"I've met Anissa."

"When? Or better yet, how?"

Justin told the story.

"So, they have you doing roadwork?"

"Yeah. Gets me outside the prison, at least."

"I'm sure that helps."

"Hey, how is Kyrsten?"

"She's doing well with her tutoring. She has made quite a few friends. Anissa is scheming to get her over her fear of horses."

"Yeah, I'd heard she got scared after the accident. Hopefully she conquers that."

"I believe she will. It'll just take time and alot of courage on her part."

"Does she still listen to music alot?"

"Yes, she has quite the extensive playlist, and it's almost always on at her house."

"How's Madison. She only ever says she's good."

"She doesn't want to worry you, likely. She has a stay-at-home job. Did she tell you that?"

"Yes. Does she like it?"

"She does seem to, actually. She's excited about Kyrsten's progress. She's still trying to figure out how to clear you."

"She doesn't have to worry about that. I told her I have a friend looking into it."

"She misses you, Justin."

"I know."

"Has the deputy found anything?"

"Not that I know of. Hey, I have to go."

"Alright. Praying for you."

"Thanks. For everything."

"Bye, Justin."

Kathlyn set down her phone, hoping fervently her cousin would be released soon.

Chapter 17: Unseen Victory

For the LORD your God is He that goeth with you, to fight for you against your enemies, to save you. ~Deuteronomy 20:04

"Sorry, I'm late." Kathlyn entered DJ's bedroom. "I had a meeting that ran longer that I expected."

"No problem." DJ gestured for her to have a seat.

Everyone else was already there, including the two boys.

"First order of business: the boys need names," Katya declared.

"Names?" David raised an eyebrow.

Katya quickly explained; then, she introduced herself. "I'm Kaari. Hilary is Hira, Anissa is Anela, Kyrsten is Kyrsi. DJ refused a name, and Kathlyn just uses her middle name, which is Eirdis."

"So, why do DJ and Kathlyn get to break the rules?" David asked.

"DJ didn't want another nickname since 'DJ' is already a short-form of her real name. Kathlyn couldn't figure out a nickname using the regular criteria." Hilary shrugged.

"So, if Kathlyn can just use her middle name, can we also? Alyosha glanced at Katya.

"How long are y'all's middle names? 'Cause Eirdis is actually one letter too long." This came from Anissa.

"David's is the right length," DJ interjected.

"What is it?" Anissa insisted.

David supplied, "Niall."

"Alyosha's is two letters too long," Katya spoke up. "But I can't figure out a name for him otherwise, either."

"I wondered if you remembered my middle name." He grinned.

"Of course." Katya was slightly indignant.

"Technically, since the b and h combine, we could count them as one letter if you like. "Cause together, they sound like a v."

Katya contradicted, "But it's not one letter. And if you're gonna do it like that, then the i and o would count together too."

Alyosha rolled his eyes.

Kathlyn chuckled. "Would either of y'all like to include us in the debate?"

"My middle name is Siobhan." Alyosha proceeded to spell the name.

DJ raised her eyebrows. "That is the weirdest name I have ever heard."

Kyrsten giggled.

"It's Irish." Alyosha shrugged.

"I thought you were Russian." Hilary frowned.

"I am, but my middle name's not."

"David's name is Scottish if it's spelt the way I think it is," Katya commented.

David spelt it aloud.

She nodded in confirmation. "Scottish."

"I vote the boys use their middle names," Kyrsten put in suddenly.

The others agreed.

"Welcome to the group, Niall and Siobhan," Kathlyn smiled warmly.

"Does everyone have a favorite Bible Verse?" Kyrsten introduced the topic.

"You first," Anissa nudged her.

"Psalms 43:03," she stated simply.

"Mine is 01 Peter 05:07," DJ responded.

Hilary went next. "Jeremiah 17:07."

"01 Thessalonians 02:12." Katya smiled.

"I really like Isaiah 35:04," David declared.

"Proverbs 16:20." Kathlyn looked at Anissa.

"I don't have one." Anissa avoided the question.

Alyosha was last. "My favorite is Jeremiah 31:03."

Anissa's sharp intake of breath was not lost on Kyrsten. "You okay?" Kyrsten whispered.

"What does Jeremiah 31:03 say?" Anissa asked Alyosha shakily.

Alyosha quoted, "'The LORD hath appeared of old unto me, saying, Yea, I have loved thee with an everlasting love: therefore with lovingkindness have I drawn thee.'"

Anissa closed her eyes.

"Anela, are you okay?" Hilary's voice was filled with concern.

"I'm fine, I just…" she opened her eyes again, "I had to memorize that as a kid. My Dad helped me," her voice dropped to a whisper on the last sentence.

Kyrsten threw her arms around Anissa. "Wouldn't that make the Verse special?" she murmured.

Anissa took a slow breath. "I didn't remember all of it. I…"

Alyosha leaned forward, putting his elbows on his knees. "How close are you to God?"

Everyone except Kyrsten and Anissa stared at him.

"Just because she doesn't remember all of a Verse, it doesn't mean she isn't close enough to God," DJ reasoned.

"We're supposed to be accountability partners, right?" Alyosha glanced at Katya.

Katya nodded slowly.

"Then my question to Anela remains," he persisted, facing forward again.

Anissa finally answered, "I'm… I'm not."

"I knew that," Kyrsten whispered.

"Do you *believe* in God?" DJ suddenly remembered how noncommittal Anissa had been on the riding trip. Now, it made sense.

"I have believed in God since I was young, but I'm not *close* to Him."

"Why not?" DJ countered.

Anissa did not respond.

"Is it because He took your dad away?" Hilary ventured. She had heard of similar situations before from various people.

Anissa lowered her head. She didn't have to answer; they all knew Hilary was right.

"Anissa—" Alyosha began.

"Don't," she interrupted. "Don't tell me he's in a better place. It doesn't help."

Alyosha raised his hands in a conciliatory gesture. "I wasn't going to say that. I was just going to say that no matter what, God still loves you, and He *does* work all things for good, although we don't always see it. I would just advise you to search the Bible for the answers you need. And I will be Praying for you."

"We'll *all* be praying for you," Hilary added.

"You know, alot of times, if we walk away from God, we feel like we're too far gone to ever go back by the time we realize our mistake. But the reality is that He never leaves us nor forsakes us, no matter how many bad decisions we make. The Bible says in Psalms 139:07-08, 'Whither shall I go from Thy Spirit? Or whither shall I flee from Thy presence? If I ascend up into Heaven, Thou art there: if I make my bed in hell, behold Thou are there'." Kathlyn continued, "Two guys I know did a demonstration one time. First, they showed our mentality about God: the one walked away from his partner one step at a time until he was so far it seemed he could never return. Then, they showed God's reality: the guy started stepping away, and his partner stayed close behind him the entire time, so when the first guy turned around, his partner was right there waiting for him."

Anissa felt tears building behind her eyelids as she pictured the scene Kathlyn described. Truly? Did God really remain that close even after so long? "But why did He take my Dad?" she choked out.

Kathlyn got up and sat beside Anissa. She put an arm around the girl's shoulders. "I don't know why God decided to take your daddy Home when He did. I'm so sorry I can't answer that. But I know God loves you, and I know that your dad is safe. And I truly believe God will use all this for something miraculous in your life."

"The only miracle I want is my Daddy." Anissa could no longer hold back the tears.

"I know you do, Sweet Girl." Kathlyn hugged her close.

Kyrsten threw her arms back around Anissa, and she and Kathlyn remained there as the rest of the group gathered around. The others laid their hands on Anissa, and Alyosha prayed aloud for God to reveal Himself to Anissa and for peace about her dad.

"Thanks, Y'all," Anissa whispered after the prayer.

DJ shot Kathlyn a grin. It was something at least.

After the meeting, Kathlyn offered to drive Kyrsten home to save her mother, who had been driving the girl to each meeting, a trip. Kyrsten agreed.

They were in Kathlyn's Jeep before Kyrsten asked, "Do you think I'll ever be able to bike back and forth for hangouts like the others?"

"Of course; you would just have to always have a buddy with you. Like Anissa could ride to your house; then y'all bike to mine together, for example. I'm sure, any of them would be willing to bike with you. This is obviously provided that your mother agrees."

"So, I *could* bike as long as I had a buddy?"

"Absolutely. We just need to get you back on a bike either in a parking lot or a longer driveway at first until you're comfortable. Then we can get you on the road with an adult; then finally move to just a buddy. The biggest thing is you will have to get the feel of keeping it straight and learn how to negotiate turns. Then the buddy would warn you of things to watch out for, and tell you when to turn," Kathlyn explained.

"I want to try it soon."

"I'll talk to your mom. First order of business is to buy you a bicycle."

Kyrsten grinned.

"Speaking of, well, sorta; you know what else you can do blind with a buddy?"

Kyrsten cocked her head to the side. "What?"

"Horseback riding."

Kyrsten shook her head vigorously. "No way."

"Why not? You would have me, Anissa, and others there to help you and keep you safe. The horse isn't going to hurt you; we'd put you up on Indie. Or Anissa has offered for you to ride Rawad. Both are really calm and well-trained. You won't get hurt again." Kathlyn tried to think of a different way to convince the girl.

"How can you promise I won't get hurt?"

Kathlyn pressed her lips together. Kyrsten had her there. The girl was smart.

"Horses remind me of the worst day of my life; I never want to ride again."

She made one last attempt. "Maybe one good ride could help change what you associate them with?" She

155

hated that the desperation could be heard in her voice. Not very professional.

"You sound like Anissa or DJ," Kyrsten stated.

Kathlyn sighed. "I know. Just think about it, okay?"

Kyrsten remained silent.

Monday, August 01

Kyrsten stayed close to Kathlyn's side as they walked through the store. She, Kathlyn, and her mom were there to find a bike for Kyrsten.

"Here are the bikes," Madison announced.

"Even though she can't ride it, she'll need to at least sit on it, so we know we're getting the right size," Kathlyn said.

Madison agreed.

Kyrsten just listened as the two adults discussed the bikes available before finally settling on one that should work perfectly, except they could not reach it.

"I'll go ask a worker to get it down for us." Madison left.

"Is the rack too high to reach?" Kyrsten asked Kathlyn.

"Yes. The bike's on the very top. And most of the others will be the wrong size for you."

Madison returned with a worker following her. "That one," she told him, pointing to the bike.

The worker nodded. "I'll grab a ladder. Wait here a moment." He walked away.

Kyrsten started singing while they waited,

> *You're my victory*
> *Reason why I sing*
> *Everything I need*
> *There's no other Name*
> *That deserves all praise*

When the worker came back with a ladder, he heard her singing. "You have a right pretty voice there, Girly." He set up the ladder, and climbed up it to pull the bike off its rack. He handed the bike down to Kathlyn. "There y'all go."

"Thank you." Kathlyn set the bike down and held it stable. "Kyrsten, come sit on it."

Kyrsten allowed Madison to guide her to the bike and help her to sit on it.

"She can ride it to the end of the aisle and back," the worker offered.

"She hasn't ridden in years," Madison said by way of explanation.

"I might hit something," Kyrsten added.

"It's not that hard." The worker didn't understand.

"I can't see," Kyrsten said softly.

"You're blind?"

"Yes, she is." Madison helped her daughter back off the bike.

"This one should work well." Kathlyn smiled.

"What color is it?" Kyrsten asked.

"Navy blue. That alright?"

Kyrsten nodded.

"She really can't see," the worker murmured to himself.

Madison turned to the worker. "Thanks for your help."

"No problem." He folded up his ladder as they began to walk away. "Wait!" he called. "I heard you singing earlier. How can you sing about victory when you're blind? There's no victory in that."

"Jesus is my Victory. He is the Light in darkness. He has rescued me and given me what I need to live without sight. That is a victory. I sing about victory in Him. It serves as a reminder of what He did on the Cross, too," Kyrsten replied.

"That is some amazing faith, Girly."

Kyrsten beamed.

"See, you're already making an impact," Kathlyn told her when they'd walked away.

"That's all God, not me," Kyrsten did not know how else to respond. A moment later, she began to sing again,

> *There's nothing I want more*
> *To see You high and lifted up*
> *There's nothing more powerful*
> *Than Your Name, Your Name*
> *You're my victory*
> *Reason why I sing*
> *Everything I need*

Chapter 18: Manifestation

Sylacauga, Alabama   **Tuesday,**
                                                   August 02, 2016

If I take the wings of the morning, and dwell in the uttermost parts of the sea; Even there shall Thy hand lead me, and Thy right hand shall hold me. If I say, Surely the darkness shall cover me; even the night shall be light about me. ~ Psalms 139: 09-11

Jordan checked caller ID before answering his phone. It was the detective-in-charge for Justin's case. "Hello." Jordan grimaced when he heard the eagerness in his own voice.

"Sorry it took me so long to get back to you."

"You find anything?"

"Yeah. I did. You actually provided us with a valuable lead. While we haven't found the actual perpetrator yet, we do have enough to prove Levine's innocence."

"You do?" Jordan couldn't help it; he was excited. All his hard work was finally paying off.

The detective chuckled. "Yes, we do. We'll take it before the judge as soon as we can, but he's in the middle of a huge court case right now."

"Let me know as soon as y'all are taking it to him and what he decides."

"Yeah, I will."

"Alright, thank you."

"Sure." The detective hung up.

Jordan pumped his fist in the air. "Yes!" *Finally!* He grinned widely.

Shorter, Alabama:

Anissa sighed in relief when her uncle ended their jumping lesson that day. He had worked her and Rawad much harder than in previous lessons. They needed the work, she knew, but jumping was more tiresome than dressage. Of course, since dressage was her favorite discipline, she put extra work into it anyway. Jumping was still fun, though.

"You did good, 'Nissa." Liam grinned up at her. "You head on in. I hear Kathlyn's got you on tack-cleaning today."

"Yeah. I have all my other chores done already, at least."

Liam nodded. "Have fun. Maybe I'll be able to come help in a little bit."

"Okay." Anissa left the arena and headed to the barn with Rawad clip-clopping behind her. In the barn, she made quick work of untacking and grooming Rawad. After being sure he had hay and water, she grabbed his gear and walked with it to the tack room.

Since Kathlyn was having her clean tack anyway, Anissa figured she might as well go ahead and clean Rawad's gear too.

She flipped over a large sturdy bucket to sit on and got to work. As she worked, the last meeting the group had held came to her mind. She thought about the things that Kathlyn and Alyosha had said. She knew they were right, but it was so hard! She wanted a reason for her dad's death.

But did she truly believe that would make it better? Easier to handle?

If she were honest with herself, no, she did not.

Anissa felt tears filling her eyes. Her daddy had been the one to lead her to Christ in the first place. He would be so disappointed to see her apathy throughout the previous years. And she knew full well that life was better to walk *with* God, not away from Him.

She had walked so far. Was Kathlyn right? Had He truly been right there this whole time? Reflecting back over her life, she knew He had, although she did not understand it.

"God," she began, "I'm sorry. I shouldn't have walked away. I don't know why You took my Daddy, but I know Daddy served You faithfully. I want to be like Daddy, just like him. I want the faith and peace Kyrsten has. Kathlyn says You never leave us. I want to have a relationship with You again. I love You, and… I know You Love me. Please forgive me." She stayed quiet for several minutes.

"Anissa? Why are you crying?" Uncle Liam knelt beside her and put a strong arm around her shoulders.

"I'm okay," she whispered.

"What's going on?" He sounded concerned.

Anissa met his eyes. "I left my relationship with God when He took Daddy away. And now, I just repented."

Liam embraced her. "Thank You, God. I'm so glad, Anissa. And your daddy would be so proud. In fact, I'm sure he's rejoicing right this moment."

Anissa pulled back to look him in the face. "You think so?"

"I know so," Uncle Liam stated firmly.

Anissa smiled and leaned into him again. "Your hugs remind me of Daddy's hugs."

"Is that a good thing?"

"Very good."

Wednesday, August 03

Kyrsten and Madison were in the kitchen together when Anissa arrived that morning.

Anissa stared at the kitchen table. There were at least fifty pencils of assorted colors spread out in the middle of the table. Madison and Kyrsten sat across from each other with the pencils between them. "What are y'all doing?"

"Mom's helping me organize all my colored pencils. She bought a case that has individual slots for the pencils," Kyrsten explained.

Anissa noticed the case Kyrsten spoke of sitting to Madison's right. She slid into the seat beside Kyrsten. "Do you need help?" she asked Madison.

"If you want to help me sort them by color, that would be great. As you can tell, we're just now getting started. I want to put them in the case in rainbow order since that's something Kyrsten already has memorized."

"Rainbow order?" Anissa raised an eyebrow.

"Red, orange, yellow, green, blue, indigo, violet. The colors of God's rainbow. We'll also sort the ones of the same color group from lightest to darkest."

"What about colors outside of the rainbow? Like black, brown, grey, and pink."

"I haven't figured that part out yet," Madison admitted.

Kyrsten thought about this. "Pink could be right after purple, since those are often used in combination. Then I guess, brown, black, and grey could follow after that, and I'll just have to remember it," she decided.

"We can do that," Madison agreed.

"How was the afternoon with your mom yesterday?" Kyrsten turned to Anissa.

Anissa's mom had gotten the afternoon off the day before, so Anissa had gone home instead of staying with Kyrsten.

"It was good. I always like the days she gets to spend more time with me. I often miss the days when she was always home."

"I'm glad you got to spend the afternoon with her, but I also missed you yesterday."

"Speaking of, there's something I need to tell you. Something that happened yesterday," Anissa began.

"And I'm the last to know, aren't I?" Kyrsten's tone was disapproving.

"The group doesn't know except for Kathlyn. I told her before going home yesterday."

"What is it?"

"Yesterday, while I was cleaning tack, … I recommitted my life to God."

Kyrsten squealed. "Oh, Anissa! Thank You, thank You, thank You, God!!"

Anissa laughed at her exuberance as Kyrsten threw her arms around her friend.

"I'm so glad, Anissa!!"

"At least I know how to make you happy," Anissa teased.

Kyrsten rolled her eyes as the girls separated.

"Good for you," Madison congratulated.

Anissa shrugged. "Thanks." She got back to work helping Madison with the pencils. "So, why do the pencils have to be organized now? Haven't you had them for like *ever*?"

"Some of them are new. Besides, since I can't see, they haven't been used for like ever," Kyrsten retorted.

"But you can't see now either." Anissa was clearly confused.

"No, but Mr. Dobrynin gave me tactile coloring books to use them with."

"Tactile?"

"The lines are raised so that Kyrsten can locate them by touch," Madison explained. "The pencils have to be organized precisely, so that Kyrsten can locate the specific colors she wants to use."

"Okay, so how do you know what colors to use without looking at it?"

Kyrsten tapped her forehead and grinned. "I may have lost my sight, but I haven't lost my imagination. I remember what colors go best together. As far as distinguishing the separate objects by touch, it'll just take some practice." She shrugged.

"Well, if there's anything I can do to help, just let me know. Although, I don't know much about any form of art."

"Sounds good. We'll figure it out eventually."

Madison looked up and grinned at her daughter.

"How did the lesson with Mr. Dobrynin go, yesterday?" Anissa changed the subject.

Kyrsten looked thoughtful. "It went good. He already has me writing full paragraphs. Some, he dictates what I should write; for others I have to read the paragraph and copy it down. I struggle with reading still. The raised letters are easier than the braille, but both are hard. I mess up alot."

"But you're still learning," Madison interjected encouragingly.

"I did write a whole letter to Daddy by myself after the lesson." Kyrsten sat up straighter. "All Mr. Dobrynin did was look over it after the fact to be sure it was clean and legible."

"Awesome!"

"Your daddy will love it," Madison commented, as she started inserting red pencils into the slots in the designated case.

"Yeah, he will."

Kyrsten beamed.

"I can't believe your mom agreed to have this many people here," Anissa commented to Hilary, as she looked around.

"Surprisingly, it did not take much convincing. I think she misses all the gatherings her family had in Russia. And it does help that every family is contributing to the meal."

DJ joined them. "Hilary, this is the best idea you've had yet."

Hilary shook her head in amusement.

Kathlyn and Hilary had managed to work out the get-together with everyone, although finding a day all the adults were free had been tough. Hilary was glad it had finally worked.

"Alright, Y'all. Time to come to get food," Dora announced loudly.

Hilary caught David's attention as he was passing her. "You need to hurry up and get in line before it's all gone."

"Before what's all gone?" He stood in front of her.

"Why, the creamed zucchini and microwaved fish, of course." She smirked.

"The *what?*" Anissa stared at Hilary.

DJ started laughing.

"Good one," David said before continuing to the now-forming line.

Hilary explained to Anissa, "When I first met David, he told me his mother had made us creamed zucchini and microwaved fish for supper. At the time, I almost believed him."

"That's disgusting." Anissa gave a mock shudder making Hilary grin.

The three girls got in line behind Alyosha and Katya.

"The group needs to all sit together." Katya turned to look at them. "That way we can easily hangout, and all the adults can talk about whatever it is adults talk about."

"You're not too far from being an adult yourself, you know." Alyosha playfully poked her in the ribs.

"I'm seventeen."

"Exactly. And you'll be eighteen come January."

"You *are* eighteen; you're an adult. Do *you* wish to discuss boring topics with them?" Katya put her fists on her hips.

DJ leaned closer to Hilary. "Do they always argue like this?"

Hilary smiled. "Yes."

"Not everything adults talk about is boring. You yourself get along really well with people of all ages; you find plenty to talk about." His tone was teasing. "And for the record, no, I don't wish to sit elsewhere."

Katya rolled her eyes at him. "What. Ever."

"Kathlyn's an adult." Hilary interjected.

"That doesn't count." Katya turned to her sister.

"How come?"

"Same way Alyosha doesn't count."

"Aha! I got you!" Alyosha crowed. "I knew it!" He grabbed her in a bear hug very suddenly.

Katya shrieked, momentarily caught off balance.

Several adults looked to see the source of the commotion.

"Y'all good?" Dave called.

"Yes!" Katya laughed.

Later during the meal, DJ leaned closer to Hilary to say, "I believe your idea has been met with success."

Hilary nodded, looking around. "I'm glad. This is fun. And if all our parents are good friends, then it's likely we'll *all* get to hangout more."

"Speaking of hanging out." DJ looked across the table to Kyrsten. "Kyrsten, now that you're able to do more, you need to come to youth with us."

"But that's not fair!" Anissa cried.

"Why not?" Hilary frowned.

"Because, we go to two separate campuses, and I don't get to see her on Sundays. I hoped she would go to youth with *me*."

"Why don't you just come with us?" DJ didn't see the problem. "Sylacauga is further away than Montgomery, but you're here alot on Wednesdays anyway. Just ride with us."

"I can't."

"Why?"

"Don't you remember we get back really late? That would be alot of the problem," Katya considered.

"Even if Kyrsten goes with her, they'll still get back late," Hilary replied.

Kathlyn jumped in. "It would be too late for Kyrsten to go with Anissa *and* for Anissa to go with us. Either way. Anissa also can't go with us because it would cause difficulties with Liam and Carrie. Keep in mind that Anissa is rarely here into the evenings on Wednesdays. Liam often takes her home, or if Carrie can, she'll come get Anissa."

"So, what do we do about youth night?" Hilary asked.

"Kyrsten would come with us, but Anissa would have to stay in Sylacauga." DJ looked to Kathlyn for confirmation.

Kathlyn shook her head. "In the future, it likely will work that way. But, correct me if I'm wrong, Kyrsten;

Kyrsten will feel more comfortable the first time if Anissa's present."

Kyrsten nodded.

"So, either Kyrsten could sleep over at Anissa's, if that worked for Carrie, or Anissa sleeps over with Kyrsten. So long as their mothers are okay with that."

"I like option two best." DJ folded her arms.

"Alyosha, you should come to youth, too," Hilary invited. "You haven't been yet."

"Sure. So long as I don't have to work."

"Does David go to youth?" Anissa glanced at him.

David responded, "Yes, with my friends."

Kyrsten listened to everything going on, glad she had so many good friends.

Chapter 19: Long-Awaited

Thursday,
August 04, 2016

Blessed is the man that trusteth in the LORD, and whose hope the LORD is. ~Jeremiah 17:07

Carrie smiled as she watched her daughter interacting with her friends. Because of Carrie's demanding job, she so rarely got to observe her daughter in daily life. When told of the plan for this gathering, Carrie'd had no idea what a treat was in store for her. On top of all that, this gathering gave Carrie a chance to get to know the people in her daughter's life, people she had only heard of up until this point.

Everyone had been very welcoming to Carrie, and had made sure she was included. She was grateful. It was also comforting knowing these people surrounded her daughter almost daily.

"I guess it's hard being unable to see her every day. With your work in Montgomery and all."

It took a moment for Carrie to realize the lady was talking to her. "Yes, it is." She turned to face the woman. Irene had a bit of an intriguing accent that Carrie had never heard before. "May I ask you a rather odd question?"

Irene smiled. "Of course."

"Where are you from originally?"

Irene chuckled. "I forget that I still carry my accent. My family and I are just used to it, I suppose."

"Used to yours, yes. Not your sister's," Simon interjected playfully.

Irene ignored her husband. "I was born in Russia, but moved here before I married Simon. My parents still live in Russia, but my sister lives in the U.S. She moved much later than I did, though."

"I did not realize you were from Russia. My daughter never mentioned it."

"I have only spent brief periods of time with her, so I am not sure she realizes. That is, unless either Hilary or Katya mentioned it, which is more than likely."

Carrie nodded.

"My daughter has a bit of an accent herself because of learning the language. She also spent several months in Russia recently."

"She did? Which daughter?"

"Katya, my oldest. As to why, well, that's a long story."

"Did your son stay there with her? I noticed his accent earlier."

Irene looked at Carrie in bemusement. "Do you mean Alyosha?"

"Yes."

"Alyosha is not my son. He moved here from Russia when Katya came home," Irene explained.

"Oh, I'm so sorry! I had no idea."

"You're totally fine."

Carrie took a bite of food, glancing over at her daughter again. "I'm so glad that not only does Anissa have good friends, she has a wise mentor in Kathlyn."

"Yes, Kathlyn has been a wonderful influence on all the girls," Simon declared.

"I second that," Dora said with a wave of her fork.

That made Carrie smile.

Friday, August 05

"One more time around, 'Nissa, and then we'll be done for the day."

Anissa nodded and gathered her reins. She nudged Rawad into a trot, and they circled the ring before moving into a canter. She pointed Rawad toward the first jump and started counting strides under her breath. They took the first jump with ease, and she immediately looked through his ears for the next one. On the second jump, Rawad's hind foot ticked the rail. It thankfully stayed in place, however. They finished the course with another tick on the last jump.

Anissa sighed. "Sorry, Uncle Liam."

"Don't beat yourself up over it. It was still a good round; you're still improving. You need to be a little more conscientious. You keep dropping him over fences. That's why you knocked the standard earlier, remember? Not only is it bad form, it's dangerous for both you and your horse." His tone was stern.

Anissa rubbed Rawad's neck. Yes, Sir."

"Alright, that's it for today. Good work." Liam left the arena.

On Anissa's way out, she was met by DJ, Hilary, and their horses. Kathlyn was not far behind them.

"Did my lesson run that late?" Anissa looked at them in surprise.

"No, Kathlyn has an important conference later," DJ explained.

Anissa nodded. "Have fun jumping."

"You really should join advanced jumping classes."

"No, thanks. I have enough trouble with *basic* jumping."

Kathlyn spoke up, "That is fine so long as you continue learning. Come on, Girls."

They entered the arena as Anissa headed to the barn.

In the arena, Kathlyn raised several of the poles on the course before outlining the agenda for that day's lesson. "Hilary, you may go first."

Hilary asked Hara for a canter, circled her, and then aimed for the first jump. When she completed the tough course without a single tick, she couldn't help shouting, "Yes!"

Kathlyn grinned in approval. "I believe that is the best I've seen from you, Hilary. Wonderful ride."

Hilary's smile only widened.

"DJ, you may go."

DJ unfortunately did not do near so well as Hilary. She knocked down the third pole. The thud of the pole rattled DJ, and she lost concentration, therefore allowing Sunshine to refuse the fourth jump.

Kathlyn crossed the arena to reset the third jump. "DJ, where is your focus? You must pay absolute attention. Do not lose your timing. Were you counting strides?"

DJ shook her head ashamedly.

"Why not?"

"I figured I should be able to time without counting strides."

"DJ, that is not how it works. Every rider counts strides. The skill is not making it obvious. Go again, and count your strides. Concentrate. You must continually urge Sunshine forward, as she is likely to refuse the same jump again."

"Yes, Ma'am." DJ did as instructed, and managed to complete a flawless ride.

"Very good," Kathlyn called.

"Thank you, Kathlyn."

Hilary grinned at DJ. "Sometimes I forget who's been riding longer, you or me," she teased.

"Yeah right. We *all* know better than that." DJ shook her head.

Hilary stuck out her tongue.

"Okay, Girls, let's get back to work," Kathlyn clapped once.

Jordan stared at his phone in amazement. How had he not seen the text until now? It had been sent a little over an hour ago.

Heading to speak with the judge, now.

He sincerely hoped the judge signed the release. This meeting would be extremely crucial for Justin.

Jordan started to set his phone down, but it began to ring. "Hello?"

"Hey, we just finished speaking to the judge."

"Did he sign the release?"

"You know I really like that judge. Doesn't make snap decisions; really thinks through all the details, he does."

"Did he sign it?" Jordan repeated.

"The lawyer's already been notified, although he did not seem to care. If he did *his* work properly, maybe Justin's imprisonment would have never happened."

"Did. He. *Sign.* It."

"I have some papers in my hand. They sure do bear the judge's signature. Plain and clear."

"So, he signed it?!" Jordan found his keys and grabbed them.

"You *might* want to head down to Atmore. Yeah, he signed it."

Jordan was already out the door. "Yes! Thank you so much."

"You're welcome." The detective hung up.

Jordan cranked his work SUV and got on the road to Atmore. He had never really minded the drive on previous trips, but current anxiety made the drive seem interminably long.

Finally, he pulled into an empty parking space at the state prison. He had to remind himself to act naturally as he left his vehicle. Bounding in there like a five-year-old on sugar was not very professional. Especially since he was still in his sheriff's uniform.

Atmore, Alabama:

Justin stood up when the guard began unlocking the cell door. Maybe he had a visitor today? That sure would be nice.

"Let's go, Levine. Change into these, and grab all your belongings." The guard handed him the clothes he'd been wearing the day he was arrested.

"My belongings?" Justin stopped in surprise.

The guard just grunted.

Justin did as ordered and followed the guard in wonder. The guard handed him some papers before leading him toward the admin.

After scanning the papers, Justin realized what they were: discharge papers, signed by the warden. Was he truly being released?

Justin had to hand over his papers at admin. for them to be double-checked. Once he had the papers in his hands again, all of his personal effects—the things taken from him when he had been arrested—were returned.

The guard then led him through a doorway into a gated area outside the building, though still within the compound. Once the door closed behind them, the guard had him proceed alone through the first gate. That gate closed, and he went through another.

"Justin!" Jordan was waiting just beyond the second gate.

"Jordan!" They clasped each other hand-to-forearm. "So, I'm really free?" Justin asked in amazement.

"Welcome to freedom, Justin. I'm so sorry this took so long."

The two men had to walk through yet another gate before Justin was truly outside the prison. He took a deep, appreciative breath. "Smells better out here."

Jordan laughed. "Yeah, it does. Come on, my vehicle's this way." They walked to the parking area. "We can put your stuff on the backseat."

Justin shook his head in chagrin. "I never thought I'd see the day that I'd enjoy seeing a sheriff's vehicle and riding in it."

"Yeah, but you get to ride in the front this time. Completely different." Jordan grinned as he slid into the driver's seat.

Justin got in the passenger side. "Does my family know yet?"

"Know what?" Jordan cranked the vehicle.

Justin rolled his eyes.

"As far as I know, they have no idea, but don't quote me on that."

"Okay."

"Which just makes this better, you know."

"It gets better?" Justin raised an eyebrow.

"Yes, 'cause now you get to surprise your family by just showing up."

"True." Justin considered this.

"I assume you want to go home right away. I don't know your address off the top of my head." He pulled the SUV out of the parking lot and got on the interstate.

Justin had kept one of the letters from Kyrsten for this purpose. All the others were on the backseat. "Here you go."

"Awesome, that works."

Justin watched the landscape going by with interest. "You don't know how many times I've dreamed of this day." He sighed.

"I can imagine."

"Any leads on your family?"

"Nope. I was an idiot and let the trail go cold, but I'll keep looking."

Justin spoke in a very stern tone, "Don't you ever use that word again, Jordan Keith."

"What, idiot?"

"Yes, it is very self-depreciating."

"Which is exactly why it fits what I was saying."

"Nonetheless, do not utter that word again," Justin warned.

"Order received, General. Over and out." Jordan saluted with military precision, and suddenly the two could not help but laugh.

Eventually, they passed through Montgomery, and turned towards Shorter.

Justin sobered. "I didn't really think through it till now. I don't live in Sylacauga anymore."

"So, your family moved after the arrest?"

Justin nodded. "I have a cousin in Shorter who promised to help my family. I've never even been to Shorter."

Jordan was surprised. "You've *never been* to Shorter before?!"

Justin shook his head no.

"Wow. Well then, welcome to the home you've never known."

Justin snorted. "Great tour guide, you are."

"I've driven through Shorter, but never stopped before today." Jordan shrugged.

"Are we close?"

"Yes, should be about to turn on your street." Jordan turned right. "Almost there."

"Is it crazy that I'm nervous?" Justin rubbed his hands over his knees.

"You'll be good, I'm sure." Jordan started counting the mailboxes. "Here we are," he said just before pulling into a driveway on the left. "This should be your house. So, welcome home."

"The home I've never known, right?" Justin tossed him a grin.

"Not for much longer." Jordan switched off the ignition. "You ready for this?"

Justin swallowed. He exhaled. Finally, he nodded.

"You got this. Hey, I have an idea."

"What?" Justin paused before getting out.

"As we walk up, stay directly behind me. I'll knock, so they don't see you at first."

"A drawn-out surprise, huh?"

"Yes, that's kinda the idea."

"Okay, let's do it. And sooner than later."

Jordan chuckled and got out of his sheriff's vehicle. He started toward the door as Justin fell into step behind him.

"Here goes." Jordan fisted his hand, raised his arm, and knocked.

Chapter 20: Freedom

Ye are of God, little children, and have overcome them: because greater is He that is in you, than he that is in the world. ~01 John 04:04

"What do you think, Anissa?" Kyrsten used the end of her grey pencil to tap the page she was attempting to color.

Anissa looked over. She snorted. "I think you need more practice."

"That bad, huh?"

"It's not terrible, but it's definitely not good, either."

"Anissa Ditka!" Madison reproved.

"It's okay, Mom." Kyrsten giggled. "I appreciate her honesty, however abrasive she tends to be." She wrinkled her nose.

Madison shook her head and simultaneously rolled her eyes.

"Oh, Anissa, you should ask Mom what she agreed to this morning." Kyrsten selected a purple pencil.

Anissa frowned. "Were we trying to convince her to agree to something?"

"Kyrsten! She didn't even know?" Madison asked in fake shock.

"She does; she just doesn't remember. Tell her!"

Madison smiled. "Anissa, you are welcome to stay the night with Kyrsten on the tenth. Provided Carrie agrees."

"So we can go to youth together," Kyrsten explained.

"So, you want to go?" Anissa shifted in her set.

"As long as you're there. Besides, DJ won't leave me alone till I go at least once."

"Okay. I'll ask Mom when she gets home tonight."

"Cool." Kyrsten nodded.

They heard a knock on the front door.

"I'll be right back girls." Madison left them at the kitchen table and walked down the hall.

Madison opened the door and was surprised to see a sheriff's deputy standing there. "Hi, can I help you? What's going on?"

"Mrs. Madison Levine, I presume?"

"Yes."

"My name is Jordan Keith. I'm with the Talladega Sheriff's Department.

"Are you the deputy who's befriended my husband?"

"Yes, Ma'am. I have news for you. It's of great importance."

"Has something happened to him? Is Justin alright?" She put a hand to her throat worriedly.

Jordan looked very grave. "There has been a change in his circumstances. The judge made a new decision in his case regarding the time and grounds for his imprisonment."

"What decision??" Madison asked anxiously.

Jordan could no longer keep from grinning. "A new lead brought about a break in the case. Ma'am, your husband has been proven innocent."

Before Madison could comprehend this drastic revelation, Jordan stepped aside.

Madison's eyes widened. She shrieked and flung herself at her husband.

"Mom!" Kyrsten pushed back from the table in the kitchen. Anissa grabbed her arm protectively as the two girls rushed to the doorway. Both were scared by Madison's scream.

Anissa immediately noticed Madison tearfully embracing Justin. "Oh my goodness!" she breathed.

"What? What is it?" Kyrsten demanded to know. Although, she did not understand all the commotion, she could distinctly hear her mother crying. "Mom?"

Anissa nudged her forward. "Go to your mom. She's directly ahead of you."

Kyrsten took two tentative steps forward. There was something Anissa was not telling her. Someone was there besides her mother, but *who?*

Justin released Madison and turned towards his daughter. "Kyrsten, my Sweet Girl."

Tears brightened the corners of her eyes at the sound of *his* voice. "Daddy?" she whispered, taking another step forward.

Justin wrapped both arms around her. "I'm home, Kyrsten. I'm finally home."

Kyrsten clung to him. "Thank You, Jesus," she whispered.

Anissa watched the emotional reunion from a distance. She could imagine how Kyrsten felt. She'd give just about anything to just be able to *hug* her daddy again; let alone to have him *home* again.

Both Madison and Kyrsten had been praying for a miracle; this was definitely it.

After the initial round of hugs and exclamations was over, Jordan told Justin a brief goodbye before taking his leave.

The happy family gravitated towards the kitchen with Anissa quietly trailing behind. She felt like an interloper in the midst of the homecoming.

The Levines sat down at the kitchen table, and Justin's attention was caught by Kyrsten's still-open coloring book.

While Kyrsten explained tactile coloring to her dad, Anissa approached Madison and spoke quietly in her ear, "May I borrow your phone to call my Uncle? He can come pick me up so that your family can just enjoy the rest of the afternoon together."

Madison shifted in her chair to see Anissa's face better. You sure?"

"Yes, Ma'am."

Madison pointed to the kitchen counter. "It's over there."

"Thank you." Anissa grabbed the phone and left the room with it. She sat down on the bottom step and dialed her uncle's number. The call went to voicemail and she blew out a frustrated breath. She dialed Kathlyn's number instead.

"Hey, Madison!" Kathlyn picked up almost immediately.

"Kathlyn, it's Anissa."

"Hey, you need something?"

"Can either you or Uncle Liam come get me?"

"Sure, but why?"

"Kyrsten's dad just got home, and I don't want to intrude."

"Justin has been released?!" Kathlyn was amazed.

"Yes, Ma'am."

"I'll be right over, okay?" Kathlyn promised.

"Thanks, Kathlyn." Anissa hung up. She decided to wait there on the steps until Kathlyn arrived. She would return the phone when she told Kyrsten and Madison goodbye.

True to her word, Kathlyn arrived in only a few minutes. After letting Kathlyn in the door, Anissa went to the kitchen to say her goodbyes. She set Madison's phone back on the counter.

Justin looked up. "Kathlyn, hey!" He stood.

Kathlyn hugged him. "Welcome home, Cousin. I'm so happy for you!"

Justin grinned. "What are you doing here?"

While Kathlyn and Justin were talking, Anissa hugged Madison goodbye, before moving around the table to where Kyrsten sat.

"I just came to pick up Anissa," Kathlyn responded.

"Are you leaving?" Kyrsten accepted Anissa's hug.

"Yeah, so that you can focus on your dad. I'll see you either tomorrow or Monday."

"Okay, love you. Don't forget to ask your mom about youth."

"Okay, love you, too." Anissa walked over to Kathlyn.

"You ready to go?" Kathlyn asked.

Anissa nodded.

"It was nice to see you again." Justin smiled at Anissa.

"Yes, Sir."

"See you at church, Justin." Kathlyn's eyes sparkled. She left with Anissa.

"I'm so glad he's free," Kathlyn declared as she pulled her Jeep out of the driveway.

"Me too. Kyrsten is ecstatic. Madison answered the door. When she saw him, she shrieked, and it scared me and Kyrsten."

Kathlyn chuckled. "I would have loved to see that."

Anissa smiled.

"How are you? You look a little down," Kathlyn observed.

"I'm glad for Kyrsten; I really am. She's the best friend I have. I just… I've always felt included almost like family there. But now that he's home, I feel like an interloper. She barely noticed when I left. She should be totally focused on her dad, but…" Anissa let her words trail off.

"Still hurts, right?"

Anissa nodded.

"I understand. That's hard. It's probably harder because of knowing your daddy can't come home." Kathlyn put into words the very pain Anissa felt.

Anissa fought the tears building behind her eyes.

"Anissa, no matter what, Kyrsten still loves you. You have not been displaced. After everything settles down, I'm sure Kyrsten will be begging to have you over every day again.

"I hope so," Anissa whispered.

Kathlyn smiled sympathetically. "Kyrsten's love for you has not changed, I promise."

They arrived at the stable, and Kathlyn parked her Jeep. "I believe the girls are still here if you want to hang out with them. Your uncle was stacking a hay shipment when you called. I don't know if he's done yet or not. Or you can stay with me."

Anissa shrugged. "I'll find my Uncle first. Maybe I can help with the hay. Should I tell DJ and Hilary about Justin, or wait till Kyrsten does?"

"I believe you can go ahead and tell them."

"Okay."

Kathlyn headed to her office, while Anissa went in search of her uncle. He was in the hay loft, as Kathlyn had predicted.

"Hey, 'Nissa. What are you doing here?" Her uncle looked up in surprise.

Anissa explained quickly. As she spoke, she helped him stack the new hay bales without being asked.

"Thanks for your help," he said once they had finished.

"You're welcome." They descended from the loft.

"Liam, Anissa, I need y'all to saddle up." Kathlyn approached them.

"Why?" Anissa noticed the tack in Kathlyn's arms, Kathlyn's personal tack.

Kathlyn grinned. "We're going for a trail ride. DJ and Hilary are coming, too."

"Really?"

"Come on, 'Nissa." Liam grabbed her hand and they hurried to the tack room.

Both saddled their horses in record time. Together, they led their horses outside to meet Kathlyn, DJ, Hilary, and their horses.

"Let's go!" Kathlyn mounted her Morgan, Arden.

There was an old trail behind Kathlyn's stable that was rarely used. That, of course, just made it more of an adventure.

The trail was wide enough for two riders beside each other, so Anissa rode up front with Kathlyn, DJ and Hilary behind them, and Liam took up the rear.

"I didn't know you could just ride off like this," Hilary commented to Kathlyn."

"Not normally. But one of the workers promised to keep an eye on things till we get back. I figured a little fun was in order."

"I'm glad. This *is* fun." DJ shifted her reins to one hand.

"See, you girls aren't the only ones with all the ideas," Kathlyn teased.

"Touché." DJ grinned.

"Doing better?" Kathlyn asked Anissa.

"Yes, definitely. Thanks, Kathlyn."

"Anytime."

As they rode, Anissa felt the former sadness lifting off her shoulders. Kathlyn was right; some fun had indeed been needed.

"Did Anissa tell y'all the news?" Kathlyn queried DJ and Hilary.

"What news?" Hilary checked Hara's stride. "Hara had come close to crowding Rawad in front of her.

"Kyrsten's dad just got released."

"That's awesome!" "Alright!" The girls' exclamations overlapped each other.

"So, *that's* why you came back to the stable." Hilary smiled.

Anissa nodded. "You got it."

Sunday, August 07

Kyrsten had gotten up early on Sunday. She was so excited to be going to church with her daddy again. Saturday, the day before, had been awesome. Sadly, she had not gotten to see Anissa, and she realized her friend had stayed at the stable all day, so that Kyrsten had more time alone with her dad. She appreciated the sacrifice on Anissa's part, but she needed to be sure Anissa realized it would not be necessary tomorrow. She wanted to spend time with her dad *and* Anissa each day, not just one of them.

Kyrsten was exuberant when they walked into the church. This Sunday would be incredible!

The Levines sat in the normal place with Kathlyn, the Seawrights, and the Devins.

Kathlyn lost no time in introducing everyone to Justin, and they all congratulated him on his recent release.

Kyrsten grabbed her dad's arm suddenly during worship when the second song started.

"What is it?" he spoke in her ear.

"This is the song! My favorite song!"

"'Tremble'?" he remembered her letter about it.

She nodded. "By Mosaic MSC."

He smiled and hugged her close as the worship song continued.

When the song finished, he told her, "I really like it."

"Good." She grinned.

Justin inhaled deeply as the service progressed. It felt so good to be finally free, to be home again, to be at church again. The church services in prison did not even begin to compare. Yes, freedom was very sweet indeed.

Chapter 21: Conquered

Now the Lord is that Spirit: and where the Spirit of the Lord is, there is liberty. ~02 Corinthians 03:17

"Are you sure?" Kyrsten asked anxiously.

Justin assured, "Yes, Kyrsten. I'll still be here when you get back. Go to youth, and enjoy the time with your friends."

Kyrsten sighed, but nodded.

Anissa elbowed her gently. "Come on, it'll be fun! Youth night is awesome!"

Carrie had agreed to let Anissa stay over with the Levines Wednesday night, so that she and Kyrsten could go to youth together.

However, now that Justin was home, Kyrsten was reluctant to go. Between the two of them, Justin and Anissa were finally able to convince her. Just in time, too, because Kathlyn arrived then to pick them up.

"Have fun, Girls." Madison hugged them goodbye.

"We will!" Anissa waved as the two hurried out the door.

"This is gonna be awesome!" DJ exclaimed from the front passenger seat as Anissa and Kyrsten got in the back with Hilary.

Anissa grinned.

When they arrived at the church in Montgomery, Kyrsten was immediately overwhelmed by the loudness and commotion.

"You got this," Kathlyn whispered encouragingly in her ear.

Kyrsten clasped Kathlyn's hand as they proceeded into the church lobby. Anissa stayed on Kyrsten's other side.

Once everyone was seated for the message, Kyrsten felt better. The worship had been loud and crazy, but Kathlyn had thankfully stayed with her in the row of seats while the other three girls went to stand in front of the stage. Anissa had offered to stay, but Kyrsten refused.

Despite the chaos of it all, Kyrsten still enjoyed the youth night greatly. The message was awesome and very informative; the worship songs filled her with hope and excitement. She definitely wanted to come back, although she was not sure that she would ever want to stand in front of the stage. She got claustrophobic and uptight in close-pressing crowds.

That night, Kyrsten and Anissa discussed the service as they got ready for bed.

"What did you think?" Anissa turned on the bathroom faucet.

"I loved it; it was just as fun as y'all told me. Definitely overwhelming at first, though." Kyrsten rinsed off her blue toothbrush.

"Do you want to go again, next month?"

"If you can come again, yes."

Anissa dried her hands. "I'll have to ask Mom."

Justin appeared in the open doorway of the bathroom. "Y'all girls ready to get to bed, yet? It's very late."

Giggling, both girls passed him to head for Kyrsten's bedroom. Kyrsten took a minute to hug her dad goodnight before entering the bedroom.

Both girls got into bed, and Anissa turned out the light. They were in bed, but they did not fall asleep right away, as they spent quite some time talking and giggling.

The next morning, both girls entered the kitchen with yawns cracking their jaws.

Justin gave them an amused grin. "I see last night's energy has dissipated."

"I suppose they got no sleep last night; I heard them talking when I got up to use the bathroom at 2 a.m." Madison bit into her toast.

The two girls traded guilty glances as they sat down.

"Guess with all that talking last night, y'all won't have a thing to speak of today." Justin poked Kyrsten, who was beside him, in the ribs.

She squirmed. "Not at all!"

Justin chuckled. "You mean to tell me y'all aren't tired of snickering through each new scheme?"

"What schemes?" Anissa acted offended.

"We'll *never* be done!" Kyrsten laughed.

"Yeah, I knew that." Justin tickled her again before pulling her into a tight hug.

Anissa felt a pang in her chest as she watched Kyrsten lean into her dad's embrace. The whole interaction reminded her of the evenings when her daddy came home from work, and they would talk and laugh over dinner. Those evenings had been the most wonderful part of each day. She looked down at her lap, fighting emotion.

"Anissa?"

The girl looked up.

"You okay?" Kyrsten's could sense the change in Anissa's mood.

Anissa tried not to choke on her words. "I'm fine."

"What's wrong?"

"I just… I miss my Daddy. He used to interact with me the same way he does with you." She nodded at Justin.

With a look of compassion, Justin got up and came around the table to kneel by her chair. "Anissa, I heard the full story of how your dad died, and I really appreciate the sacrifice he made for Kyrsten."

Anissa sniffed.

"I understand you miss him terribly. While this is not exactly the same, while I was in prison, I would just ache to be able to put my arms around my daughter. Even for a second." He continued, looking up at her earnestly, "I know you have an uncle who's close to you, but if you ever need a second male mentor, someone to encourage you or answer questions, whatever you need, I'd be glad to help you. I know that in no way makes up for the loss of your father, however."

Anissa felt tears roll down her cheeks as she processed his words.

"What do you say?" Kyrsten looked at her friend hopefully. Her friend needed this.

"Patience, Kyrsten," Madison murmured.

Anissa took a deep breath. "Can I think about it?"

Justin nodded reassuringly. "Take all the time you need."

A few minutes later, Anissa's uncle showed up to take her to work with him.

She hugged Madison and Kyrsten. "See y'all this afternoon. Have fun with your tutor, Kyrsten."

"Okay, love you."

Anissa started to leave, but impulsively turned back to hug Justin. Not sure that was the right move, she then skedaddled out of the kitchen before a word could be said, stopping only to pick up her overnight bag and water bottle.

Surprised, Liam glanced at Justin before following Anissa out to his truck.

"You want to tell me what was going on in there?"
Liam asked as he buckled his seatbelt.

"Kyrsten's dad offered to mentor me since Daddy's
in Heaven." Anissa tried to gauge her uncle's reaction out
of the corner of her eye.

"And?" His face was blank.

"I asked to think about it."

"What's the holdup?" He started the truck and
shifted to reverse.

"Doesn't it bother you?" She sipped her water.

"Should it?"

Anissa hugged her shoulders to her ears. "You're
my mentor; you have been since Daddy died."

"The way I see it, another mentor is wise. You'll get
guidance from two different perspectives instead of just
mine."

"But I have both you and Kathlyn." Anissa could not
figure out what to do. She'd been afraid Justin's offer would
make her uncle feel replaced.

"And I'm really glad you do, but adding Justin in
won't hurt. Kathlyn is a woman, so she will give you a
woman's perspective. Perfect, especially since as a woman,
she'll understand you best. But having a man's perspective
is also great for certain issues. While I will definitely
continue to mentor you and can give you a man's view, I
also hate that I'm often busy when you need me. And I've
never been married, never had kids, etc. There are certain
things I just don't understand because of lack of
experience. Justin has more experience in the relationship
realm. And I'm sure prison also gave him quite a few hard
lessons that have made him stronger."

Anissa thought through what he said. "So, it really
doesn't bother you?"

He gave her a serious look. "Not at all. I believe this is a way that God's opening a door for you. You just need the courage to step through it."

Sunday, August 14

Kyrsten was apprehensive as Kathlyn led her down the main aisle of the stable that afternoon. Everyone except her was extremely excited about this special trip to the stable after church on Sunday.

Kathlyn and Kyrsten took a right, getting closer to their destination. The only other person in the stable was Justin, who stayed close behind his daughter. Everyone else, Madison, the group, and their respective families were waiting outside near the large outdoor ring. Kyrsten was overwhelmed at how many people had driven over just to cheer her on. She knew most of them had been hoping for this day to come, although it had been her dad who finally convinced her.

Saturday, August 13, 2016

"You can do it. Don't you want to at least attempt it?"

"No. Why does everyone want me to do this so badly? Kathlyn, Anissa, Mom, the group, now you."

"Because we so badly want to see you succeed. We don't want you to be held back by fear."

Kyrsten did not respond.

"There was a riot while I was in prison. Did Mom tell you?"

"Yes."

"I was so scared, Kyrsten. Even though I refused to participate, and did my best to stay out of the way, that did not make me safe. I had to be brave. Do you know what bravery really is?"

"Courage."

"The courage to press on or do something despite the fear threatening you. We will always have to face fear, Sweet Girl, but it is God Who gives us the strength to conquer those fears daily. In fact, Jesus already defeated fear when He died on the Cross."

"I know that, but it's so hard!"

*"You're right, it is. But those hard things are what shape
our individual characters. God never promised us easy. He does
promise to walk with us and guide us through all that we face."*
Kyrsten took a deep breath. "For you, Daddy, I'll try."
"That's all I ask."

"Here we are," Kathlyn's voice brought Kyrsten
back to the present. They stopped in front of a stall.
"Kyrsten, meet Indie. He's the calmest horse I own. He's
very sweet, and he loves new people. You wait with your
dad while I put him on a lead line and bring him out to
meet you. After that, I'll tack him up, and we'll head
outside."

Twenty minutes later, they were entering the ring
through the gate Anissa held open. The spectators, except
for Liam and Anissa, who were functioning as Kathlyn's
assistants, were required to remain outside the arena.

"Alright, Kyrsten," Kathlyn began. "I will instruct
you, walk you through what to do, while Liam assists you.
He and Anissa will both encourage you and help you
implement my instructions. Even after we get Indie
moving, Liam will walk by the horse to your left and
Anissa to your right."

Kyrsten nodded and took a fortifying breath.

"You got this. 'For God hath not given us the spirit
of fear; but of power, and of love, and of a sound mind.' ~01
Timothy 01:07," Liam quoted.

"Thanks. You're the one who put me on a horse the
first time." Kyrsten remembered when he had introduced
himself to her. His voice was not one she could ever forget.
It was deep and comforting.

"That's right. You ready to get in the saddle again,
Kiddo?"

Kyrsten forced confidence into her voice. "Sure."

"Alright, when you're ready, I'll guide your left foot into the stirrup. Then, you'll push off with your right foot and swing your right leg over the saddle and sit down. I will assist you each step." Liam first guided both of her hands to the correct places on the saddle. "Grip here."

Once she was up in the saddle, all traces of confidence fled her. The ground was so far away, what if she fell again? She could feel herself shaking. She had no idea what to do, and she could not see anything. This was a terrible idea. "I can't do it," she squeaked.

"Yes, you *can*." Anissa put her left hand on Kyrsten's right knee. "You *can* do this. Remember, 'I can do all things through Christ Which strengtheneth me.'" Anissa remembered when her mom had helped her memorize Philippians 04:13. "Short and powerful," Carrie had said.

"You totally got this, Kyrsten," Kathlyn spoke assertively. "One step at a time."

Kyrsten closed her eyes and whispered the words to "Tremble", ~Mosaic MSC under her breath.

"When you're ready, we'll ask Indie for a walk," Kathlyn instructed calmly. "You hold the reins, but allow them to rest on Indies' neck. To ask for a walk, just lightly squeeze your calves against his sides. As soon as he moves, stop the pressure."

Liam helped Kyrsten hold the reins properly. "Anissa and I will stay right beside you. Just squeeze your legs against him here." He tapped her calf muscle.

Taking several deep breaths and continuing to whisper lyrics under her breath, Kyrsten did as told. Once Indie felt the pressure against his sides through the English saddle leather, he stepped out in a walk.

"Awesome, Kyrsten!" Anissa praised. "You got it!"

Several people on the sidelines cheered.

"Now to stop, just gently pull back on the reins," Kathlyn said, after only a few minutes.

Kyrsten did so, and Indie slowed to a halt.

Kathlyn briefly explained how to ask the horse to turn with use of the legs and the reins. As she spoke, Liam demonstrated Kathlyn's words to Kyrsten by touch.

They got Indie moving again, and made a few circuits around the ring. Under Kathlyn's direction, Kyrsten herself asked Indie to turn each time.

Nearing the end of the ride, Kyrsten felt herself finally beginning to relax. In response, Indie developed more forward motion in his walk.

Anissa and Kathlyn traded grins when they saw this. Kyrsten was conquering the fear!

After another two laps, Kathlyn called for a halt. "Awesome job! I'm very proud of you, Kyrsten!!"

"Thanks, Kathlyn. Are we done?"

Kathlyn chuckled a little. "Yes, we're done. Though, you are welcome to come back anytime."

"No, thanks. That was enough." Kyrsten shook her head.

"If you want to kick your feet free of the stirrups, I'll pull you down," Liam offered. He guided her hands to his shoulders, and once her feet were free of the stirrup irons, he grabbed her around the waist and lifted her from the saddle.

Kyrsten breathed a sigh of relief when her feet touched the ground. Anissa hugged her before leading her out of the ring to her dad.

"You did it." Justin's breath whispered over her ear as he hugged her.

Justin answered the door the next day. "Jordan? What are you doing here?" He motioned for his friend to come inside.

"Sorry to drop in on you like this."

"No problem. I was just wishing for some company since Madison and Kyrsten aren't here right now. I'm guessing this is a personal visit and not work-related since you're in street clothes." Justin led Jordan to the kitchen. "Can I get you something to drink?"

"No, that's fine."

"So, what's up?" They sat across from each other.

"I need to talk."

Chapter 22: Shining Light

Arise, shine; for thy light is come, and the glory of the LORD is risen upon thee. ~Isaiah 60:01

"The detective caught the guy who framed you, yesterday. Thought you would like to know."

"Glad to hear it, but that's not why you're here." Justin leaned back in his chair.

"No, it's not." Jordan grimaced sheepishly.

"Talk to me, Jordan."

"I've been working hard to find my family," Jordan began.

"And?"

"And I've got nothing. No leads, no clues."

"Nothing at all?"

"Not anymore." Jordan rubbed his forehead.

"What do you mean 'not *anymore*'?"

"I had finally uncovered a lead. *One* lead. Led to an abandoned building."

"No clues in the building?"

"No clues, but plenty of evidence."

"What kind of evidence?" Justin was getting tired of prompting for answers. Jordan was obviously a terrible storyteller; this was ridiculous.

Jordan sighed. "I found evidence confirming that my wife was there. The lead was right. Key word: *was*. The building was vacated by the time I arrived."

"So, you keep looking."

"I have! There's nothing, Justin!" Jordan angrily got up and began to pace. "Now, I'm convinced they're both in danger, and I can't do a thing about it!"

Justin had never seen his friend this agitated before.

Jordan deflated and stopped pacing. "Maybe this is a sign I should just give up."

Justin stood and strode to his friend's side. "Absolutely not. Are you hearing yourself? You realize they're in danger, and you're gonna give up, just because one lead dead-ended? No giving up. You *will* find your family. I will continue praying for you, and will help in any other way I can." He grabbed Jordan's shoulders, and physically turned his friend to face him. "It's time you yourself started praying, too."

Jordan scoffed. "Pray to a God I don't believe in? Isn't that like hypocritical, or something?"

Justin led him back to the table, and took a seat beside him. "Do you really still not believe? The evidence is all around you."

"What evidence?"

"You've been searching for months for your family, no leads; now, you finally got one." He held up a hand when Jordan started to object. "I know it dead-ended for now, but you *still* got a lead. God gave you that lead. God protected me in prison amidst all the tension and craziness that goes on there. God showed you the discrepancy that freed me. God built our friendship. You know what else? I wish you'd been here yesterday. My daughter conquered her fear of horses. God gave her the strength for that. She's been scared since she became blind. God is everywhere, involved in everything. Open your eyes, Bro."

"What about the fact that you were falsely accused? That your daughter's permanently blind? That the lead *did* dead-end? What about that?" Jordan demanded.

Justin smiled patiently. "God works everything for good."

"You really believe that?"

"I do."

"I know you do. Even in prison, you knew
something good would come of it. I thought you might be
mentally off for a little while there."

Justin laughed. "Mentally off, huh? Well, alot of
people think Christians are crazy. Alot of *Christians* think
Christians are crazy."

"Really?"

"Oh, yeah. My daughter sings this song sometimes;
I don't know the name of it. It says something about people
thinking we're a little crazy and the singer having to agree
with them."

"That's interesting. I had no idea."

"As a Christian, you have to learn to only care what
Jesus thinks, not what others think." Justin shrugged.

"Do you think God would help me find my family if
I gave Him my life?"

"That's not for me to say. But you need to give Him
control, not because you want something *from* Him, but
because you truly want to live your life *for* Him. He's
already given you more than you need. But you have to
come to the point that you realize you can't do this without
Him, can't live life without Him. It's not a halfway thing.
You're either all in, or you're out." He leaned forward. "And
I really don't want you to be out. Believe me when I tell
you, that is not the way you wanna go."

Jordan swallowed and looked down. "Look, I can
hear the conviction in your voice. It's just really hard to
wrap my head around all this."

"I understand." Justin allowed Jordan a minute to
process all that had been said.

There was a slight commotion coming in the front
door. "We're home!" Madison called cheerily from the
entryway.

Jordan stood up quickly. "I'll let you hang with your family."

Justin protested as he also stood. "No, you don't need to leave. My family would love a chance to get to know you, and you're welcome to stay for supper. After the meal, we can continue talking."

Jordan shook his head. "Another time. I need to get back to looking for my family."

"Think about what we talked about," Justin pleaded.

Jordan gave him a quick hug. "I will. See ya."

"I'll be Praying for you."

Jordan nodded and passed Kyrsten and Madison on his way out.

Justin stared after him in dismay.

"Hey, Daddy." Kyrsten hugged him.

"Hey, Sweet Girl."

She sensed something was not right. "What's wrong?"

Justin sighed. "Jordan and I were talking about Christianity. I have been praying for his Salvation since I met him. He just came so close."

"To getting saved?" Madison set her phone down on the counter.

"Yes."

"I'll pray for him too, Daddy. Maybe God will use what you told him today to finally get through to him."

"I sure hope so."

"On a lighter note, Kyrsten is fully registered for school in Tuskegee now. She'll start Monday, the 22nd."

"Alright! You excited?" Justin grinned at his daughter.

"Yes! And no. I am, but I'm also nervous. And I'll miss Mr. Dobrynin as my tutor. However, he thinks this is the best next step, and if I end up having trouble, he'll start tutoring me on the side again."

"I'm so proud of you, Kyrsten. You will do well, I'm sure."

Kyrsten beamed.

"Yes, she has come a very long way, especially in this last year." Madison smiled proudly.

Tuesday, August 16

Kathlyn sighed as she picked up her ringing phone. The number came up as unknown. "Hello, this is Kathlyn."

"Hi. I heard that a Kathlyn Shirah at this number can take in struggling teenage girls?"

"Excuse me? Who is this?"

"Chapman Tuller, principle of the middle school in Montgomery."

"And you are calling me because…?" Kathlyn waited for Chapman Tuller to finish the sentence.

"We have an eleven-year-old girl here that is still waiting for her mother. Thus far, her mother is three hours late. According to my records, she lives in a small town called Hope Hull. A staff member drove by the house on his way home and said the place is empty. The mother has never been late before. I hate to call the police, even though that's standard procedure. I'm afraid the girl will be thrown into foster care and there's too many horror stories about that system. A friend told me you mentor teenage girls. Would you be willing to take this one in until the mother is found?"

Kathlyn was shell-shocked. "Mentoring kids at my stable is a far cry from what you're asking."

The principle sighed heavily. "I realize that, but I hoped you would make an exception."

201

"You said y'all are in Montgomery? How did you even get my information? You called my personal cell, not the stable."

"Like I said, a friend told me about you."

"Who is this friend?"

"Look, I'll explain everything in person if you would please come at least look into the situation?"

Kathlyn could not think. "Listen, I'll call you back." She hung up abruptly. *Now what? What was going on?*

"Hey, where's Kathlyn?" DJ called. She and Hilary slowly entered the ring with their horses. Instead of their instructor, Liam stood in the center of the arena waiting for them.

"Rather than cancel y'all's lesson entirely, Kathlyn asked me to give y'all a jumping lesson, or review, at my level. She had something urgent come up, and that's all I know. She left about five minutes ago. She told me to tell y'all she'd make it up to y'all later." Liam shrugged.

"Where's Anissa? Is she still here?" This came from Hilary.

"No, she left for Kyrsten's already."

"Will Kathlyn be back in time for the group meeting this evening?" DJ mounted Sunshine.

Liam shook his head. "I have no idea. She only told me that she had to leave right away and to take over y'all's lesson for her."

"This is really weird, and very not like Kathlyn," Hilary mumbled as she also mounted. She adjusted her helmet. "What do we do first?"

"I'm glad the group meeting is at my house tonight! This is gonna be fun!" Kyrsten grinned.

Anissa chuckled at her friend's exuberance. "You're silly."

"Thanks."

"Where's your dad?"

"He's upstairs with Mom, I think."

"Are they busy?"

"Let's go find out." Kyrsten got up.

Anissa followed her friend to Justin and Madison's bedroom. The door was open when they arrived.

"Hello, Girls. What's up?"

"Anissa wants to know if y'all are busy," Kyrsten stated matter-of-factly.

Anissa rolled her eyes.

Madison smiled. "Y'all can come in."

The girls climbed onto the bed with the adults. "This is how Anissa and I always talk. I didn't realize adults did that, too."

"Where do you think kids get it from, Silly?" Madison tapped her daughter's knee.

"I hadn't thought of it that way."

They all shared a laugh.

"Wait, what is that?" Kyrsten silenced them.

"I didn't hear anything." Anissa shrugged.

"Shh."

A moment later, they heard a knock on the door downstairs.

"Someone's here!" Kyrsten vaulted off the bed and hurried down the steps.

Justin watched her go. "It still amazes me how normally she functions even without sight."

"Once she decided she wouldn't let blindness stop her, it was like the light got turned back on." Madison got off the bed.

203

"God is that light in her," Justin stated seriously. "As she often says, He's the Victory in our lives."

Madison agreed. "Anissa, that's probably y'all's friends arriving. It is that time." She left the room.

"Justin?" Anissa was not ready to leave yet.

"What's up?"

"I've decided to accept your offer of mentorship, if you still want to do that."

"Absolutely." Justin hugged her. "Now, go hangout with your friends. I'll see you later."

Anissa smiled and obeyed.

"Thank You, God, for these precious girls, for freedom, and for being a shining Light in all of us," he breathed.

Downstairs, everyone had arrived, except for Kathlyn. Hilary and DJ explained what Liam had told them to the others as they all headed up to Kyrsten's bedroom.

Once they were all settled in the room with the door closed, Anissa said, "Kyrsi has exciting news, Y'all."

"What?" Katya raised an eyebrow.

Kyrsten grinned. "I registered for public school with y'all in Tuskegee yesterday."

"Awesome!" Hilary cried.

"Good for you." DJ nodded.

The door opened, and Kathlyn peeked her head in. "Am I too late to join?"

"Kathlyn!" "Where were you?" "What happened?" Several spoke at once.

"One thing at a time." Kathlyn gestured for them to calm down. "I went to Montgomery to pick up a friend. And I realize this is nonstandard, but I brought her along for this meeting."

DJ and Hilary traded questioning glances. *A friend from Montgomery?*

Kathlyn pushed the door the rest of the way open to reveal the pre-teen girl standing a little behind her. She gently nudged the shorter girl forward. "Allow me to introduce Abby Rosen, who will be my guest for a little while." She introduced the members of the group to Abby, using their real first names, and not the nicknames.

"How long have y'all known each other?" DJ asked by way of conversation.

"I don't know her," Abby spoke for the first time. She crossed her thin arms.

Katya leaned forward. "Excuse me?"

Epilogue: Perfect Timing

**Monday,
September 10, 2016**

For the vision is yet for an appointed time, but at the end it shall speak, and not lie: though it tarry, wait for it; because it will surely come, it will not tarry. ~Habakkuk 02:03

"Justin! Have you seen this?" Madison pointed to the news story on her computer screen.

Justin read over her shoulder. He whistled low. "God is incredible. I knew there was tension building there before I left."

"Tension where?" Kyrsten had just entered the living room and overheard the conversation.

"At the prison your daddy was at." Madison was still staring at the article.

"What happened?"

Justin raised his eyebrows. "Apparently, a huge prison strike just broke out last night. One month and four days after I was freed. God got me out of there before things got ugly."

"What is a strike?"

Madison explained, "The prisoners are refusing to work and rioting in protest of the conditions of the prison. They believe it to be unfair."

"I don't blame them," Justin said under his breath. "Though, I would never resort to that kind of violence." He pointed to a line of the story.

Madison caught her breath. The warden and a guard had been stabbed, and had severe injuries. Yes, God had indeed known exactly when to rescue Justin.

"I'm glad you're free, Daddy." Kyrsten sat beside him on the couch.

Justin hugged her. "Me too. Here with y'all is much better than prison." He grinned.

See Abby's story unfold in upcoming sequel *Keeping Faith* ~Elivia Kanatiquelli!

Notes:
-Chapter 14's title looks different than the word in the body of the chapter because Russian cursive changes the letters' look just like U.S. cursive does.

-Typically, the lawyer contacts the family about a prisoner's release, but it is possible that he/she neglected to do so.

-The prison strike began in Holman Correctional Facility, Atmore, Alabama on September 09, 2016. It quickly spread to multiple prisons across the United States. While, yes, both a prison guard and the warden of Holman Correctional Facility were stabbed, they were not killed. They survived and recovered well.
The riots mentioned in the book, are author's creative license. It is very likely that there was tension and minor riots before the strike itself broke out.

Songs used in this book:
"You're Here" ~Highlands Worship
(lyrics used under license Highlands Creative Publishing)

 "Tremble" ~Mosaic MSC
(note: I highly recommend listening to the live version from their album Glory & Wonder.)

"Victory" ~Highlands Worship
(lyrics used under license Highlands Creative Publishing)

"Living For The Other Side" (ft. Royal Tailor) ~Capital Kings

Pronunciation Guide –Eyes On The True Light
Anela- uh-neh-lah ---- Hawaiian
Anissa- Uh-nih-suh ---- Arabic
Ariadna- aw-r-ee-aw-d-n-a ---- Russian
Eirdis- air-DEE-s ---- Icelandic
Dinah- DEE-nah ---- Hebrew (French pronunciation)
Ditka- Dee-t-KAH ---- Czech
Dobrynin- Duh-bre-nen ---- Russian (barely roll the r)
Hara- HAHR-ah ---- Sanskrit
Hira- HIGH-rah ---- Sanskrit
Kaari- Car-ee ---- Ameru
Katya- KAH-chya ---- Russian
Kyrsi- Kee-r-see ----
Levine- Lee-vine ---- Hebrew
Niall- Nee-all ---- Gaelic
Rajiya- RAH-zhee-ya ---- Arabic
Rawad- Rah-wed ---- Arabic
Shirah- SHY-rah ---- Anglo-Saxon
Siobhan- shih-vawn ---- Irish
сторонник(storonnik)- star-on-yik ---- Russian (roll r; say
    fast; star is hard sound)
حبيب(habib)- hah-bee-bon ---- Arabic
Naerhet- NARR-het ---- Norwegian (barely roll the r)

-Meaning of names, listed in order of character's appearance:
First Names:
Rawad: Arabic meaning 'pioneer'.
Liam: Irish for 'with gilded helmet' and 'resolute protector', and
Old High German for 'with gilded helmet'.
Kyrsten: German meaning 'Christian'.
Ingryda: Polish for 'beloved; beautiful', and Germanic for
'beautiful, graceful, fair'.
Kyrsi: Scandinavian for 'amaranth blossoms', 'frost', and
'cherry', and Finnish for 'amaranth blossoms' and 'Christian'.
Madison: Old English for 'son of Matthew' and 'son of the
mighty warrior', Hebrew for 'strong fighter', 'gift of the Lord',
and 'woman from Magdala', and Old German for 'mighty in
battle' and 'child of Maud'.

Justin: Latin meaning 'just; fair; righteous' and 'upright'.
Anissa: Arabic for 'friendly', 'companion', 'faithful friend', and 'young lady'.
Elaine: Hebrew for 'my God has answered me', Greek meaning 'sun ray; shining light', and Scottish for 'bright, shining light'.
Anela: Hawaiian for 'angel', Latin for 'messenger', and Greek for 'messenger of God'.
Carrie: American meaning 'free'.
Kathlyn: Vietnamese meaning 'pure and holy beauty'.
Eirdis: Icelandic for 'merciful protector', 'protection', 'peace', 'help', 'mercy', 'sister', 'wise woman', 'seeress', and 'virgin'.
Emily: Latin for 'rival', 'strive', 'industrious', and 'flatterer'.
Cayden: Gaelic for 'son of Cadán', and American meaning 'fighter'. Also means 'battle'.
Wind: American meaning 'moving air'.
DJ: English meaning 'love an humble' or 'great leader'.
Dinah: Hebrew meaning 'judged, vindicated'.
Jane: English meaning 'God is gracious'.
Hilary: Latin meaning 'joyful, cheerful, glad'.
Rajiya: Arabic meaning 'hopeful'.
Hira: Sanskrit meaning 'diamond'.
Marlowe: Old English for 'from the hill by the lake', 'lake remains', and 'driftwood'.
Jordan: Hebrew for 'descend', and Germanic for 'to flow down', 'earth daring', and 'the river of judgement'.
Sunshine: English meaning 'light from the sun'.
Hara: hindu for 'to scize', Greek for 'joy', Hebrew for 'princess', and Sanskrit for 'seizer'.
Zane: Hebrew for 'God is gracious' and 'gift from God', and Arabic for 'beauty; grace'.
Dora: Greek meaning 'gift' or 'God's gift'.
Dave: Scottish meaning 'beloved' or 'friend'.
David: Israel meaning 'beloved' and 'son of Israel'.
Niall: Irish Gaelic meaning 'champion' and 'cloud'.
Dorothy: English meaning 'gift of God'.
Marga: Hebrew meaning 'pearl'.
Margaret: Latin for 'pearl', and French for 'cluster of blossoms'.
Daniel: Hebrew meaning 'God is my judge'.
Irene: Greek meaning 'peace'.

Simon: Hebrew meaning 'listen'.
Katya: Russia meaning 'pure'.
Ariadne: Greek meaning 'most holy'.
Kaari: Ameru for 'young girl', Eastern African for 'pure', and Finnish for 'rare excellence; precious stone'.
Alyosha: Russian for 'defender', and Greek for 'helper of the people'.
Siobhan: Irish Gaelic for 'God is gracious', and Hebrew for 'Yahweh is gracious/merciful'.
Lyle: French for 'islander', English for 'the island; from the island', and Scottish for 'someone living on an island'.
Hawk: English meaning 'hawk, a bird'.
Indie: India meaning 'blue' or 'from India'.
Arden: English for 'from the eagle valley' and 'great forest', Brythonic for 'highland', and Latin for 'ardent; fiery'.
Chapman: Old English for 'merchant, tradesperson'.
Abby: English for 'joy of the father', and Hebrew for 'my father is joyful'.

Surnames:
Ditka: Czech for 'important in war', and English for 'prosperous in war'.
Levine: Old English for 'beloved friend', and Ashkenasic Hebrew (Jewish) for 'joining'.
Shirah: Anglo-Saxon meaning 'bright'.
Norris: English meaning 'northerner'.
Devins: Irish meaning 'an ox or stag'.
Seawright: Old English for 'sea-power' or 'victory-power'.
Bauguess: Welsh meaning 'little'
Keith: Scottish meaning 'offspring', 'young person', and 'wood'.
James: Hebrew for 'he who supplanted', and English for 'a heel'.
Preobrazhensky: Russian for 'of the Transfiguration' and 'transformation'.
Dobrynin: Russian meaning 'son of Dobrynya'.
Tuller: (Middle High) German for 'fence', 'patience', 'festival', and 'elevation, knoll'.
Rosen: Jewish for 'rose(s)', and German for 'burning bush'.

213

www.ingramcontent.com/pod-product-compliance
Lightning Source LLC
Chambersburg PA
CBHW070511160726
48003CB00004B/1528